"Maybe you should stay at my place for the rest of the night."

"Thanks, but I don't really think that's necessary. If he really wanted to harm me, then he wouldn't have called to warn me off."

Hank reluctantly agreed with her assessment. "Still, you've made yourself visible and that could be dangerous."

"Then maybe we should make your services to me official," Melody replied. "I don't know what the going rate for bodyguard services is, but I might be able to afford you for a little while."

"That isn't necessary," he replied. "I'm already on board." He wanted to demand that she stop asking questions, demand that she leave the investigation to the appropriate authorities. But he didn't have the right to demand anything of her and besides, he had a feeling it wouldn't do any good.

Dear Reader,

When Hank Tyler and his little girl, Maddie, first appeared in my head I knew they had to have a special story and that meant I had to bring a special woman into their lives. Enter Melody Thompson, a woman grieving the murder of her sister, Lainie.

Natural-Born Protector is about a man learning to reconnect with his child, a woman finding forgiveness for herself, but ultimately it's about two people discovering that love has the power to heal and that there's nothing more powerful than family.

I hope you enjoy reading their story as much as I enjoyed writing it!

Happy reading.

Carla Cassidy

CARLA CASSIDY

Natural-Born Protector

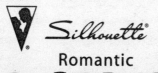

Romantic
SUSPENSE

 SILHOUETTE BOOKS

ISBN-13: 978-0-373-27597-7
ISBN-10:   0-373-27597-8

NATURAL-BORN PROTECTOR

Copyright © 2008 by Carla Bracale

Books by Carla Cassidy

Silhouette Romantic Suspense

†*Man on a Mission* #1077
Born of Passion #109
†*Once Forbidden...* #1115
†*To Wed and Protect* #1126
†*Out of Exile* #1149
Secrets of a Pregnant Princess #1166
††*Last Seen...* #1233
††*Dead Certain* #1250
††*Trace Evidence* #1261
††*Manhunt* #1294
‡*Protecting the Princess* #1345
‡*Defending the Rancher's Daughter* #1376
‡*The Bodyguard's Promise* #1419
‡*The Bodyguard's Return* #1447
‡*Safety in Numbers* #1463
‡*Snowbound with the Bodyguard* #1521
‡*Natural-Born Protector* #1527

Silhouette Books

The Coltons
Pregnant in Prosperino

†The Delaney Heirs
††Cherokee Corners
‡Wild West Bodyguards

CARLA CASSIDY

is an award-winning author who has written more than fifty books for Silhouette. In 1995, she won Best Silhouette Romance from *Romantic Times BOOKreviews* for *Anything for Danny*. In 1998, she also won a Career Achievement Award for Best Innovative Series from *Romantic Times BOOKreviews*.

Carla believes the only thing better than curling up with a good book to read is sitting down at the computer with a good story to write. She's looking forward to writing many more books and bringing hours of pleasure to readers.

Prologue

Hank Tyler sat in the chair opposite Dalton West, waiting for his old friend to make a decision about hiring him for the family business, Wild West Protective Services.

Hank had been back in his hometown, the small Oklahoma town of Cotter Creek, for the past four months, trying to decide what he wanted to do with the shambles of his life.

He hadn't just been floundering for the past four months, but rather for almost the last two years. His ranch in Texas had become a hotbed of memories too painful to endure, so despite the protests of his little daughter, he'd sold his spread and had moved himself and his daughter here to Cotter Creek for a new beginning.

"Are you sure this is what you want to do?" Dalton asked. "You realize that working for us as a bodyguard would mean you'd have to be available for travel—sometimes for weeks at a time."

"I realize that," Hank replied.

"And that won't be a problem with you as a single parent?"

"Not at all. My mother lives in a town house in the same building as mine. She'll be available to take care of Maddie whenever I'm away."

"I understand there's been some drama where you live," Dalton replied.

Hank nodded. "The woman across the hall was just murdered. Lainie Thompson—did you know her?" A knot of emotion balled up in Hank's chest as he thought of the neighbor who had become a close friend in a remarkably short time. Lainie's death was a deciding factor in Hank's decision to join Wild West Protective Services.

"Everyone knew Lainie," Dalton said, nodding. "She was a troubled woman." He leaned back in his desk chair and eyed Hank for a long moment. "I could definitely use you. Even though your military training was a long time ago, I've seen you at the shooting range and know you're well qualified. You're obviously in tip-top physical shape."

Dalton frowned thoughtfully, then continued. "These bodyguard gigs pay very well, but this isn't like working a nine-to-five job with a steady paycheck. In fact, I've got nothing for you at the present time."

"If you're worried about my finances, then don't," Hank replied. "Selling the ranch in Texas left me what some would consider a wealthy man. I'll be fine until something comes up."

Dalton stood and held out a hand to Hank. "Then welcome to Wild West Protective Services."

Hank rose and grasped Dalton's hand in a firm shake, knowing that he had just irrevocably changed his life.

Chapter 1

The man was in Lainie's bathroom, cleaning up blood from the tiled floor. Melody Thompson dropped her suitcase, stifled a scream and stumbled backward.

The stranger turned around, his handsome features registering surprise. "Wait…it's okay," he exclaimed as he scrambled to his feet. "I won't hurt you."

He was clad in only a pair of navy athletic shorts that rode low on his lean hips. And his hips were the only lean thing about him. His shoulders were broad, his chest tautly muscled, and his long legs had the athletic appearance of a man who probably jogged.

These first impressions flew through Melody's head as her body tensed with fight-or-flight energy. "Who are you?" she demanded as she backed down the hallway toward the front door.

He followed her at a nonthreatening distance as he wiped his hands on a towel. "I'm Hank Tyler." He reached into his pocket and withdrew a key ring with a single key dangling from it. "I live in the town house next door. Lainie and I were good friends. She gave me a key a couple of months ago."

The fear that had momentarily gripped her eased a bit. He did have a key and it was obvious by the fit of his jogging shorts that he was carrying no weapon.

"What are you doing in here?" she demanded. It was easy for her to translate *good friends*. Lainie didn't have male friends, but she'd always had plenty of lovers. There was no way she'd have been able to pass up this dark-haired, blue-eyed model of masculinity.

"I knew the sheriff released this place this morning and eventually somebody from the family would come in. I thought it would be easier if the…uh…mess was cleaned up."

The mess. It didn't take a rocket scientist to understand what he was talking about. The mess was her sister's blood. A wave of grief struck her, nearly buckling her knees.

"You're Melody, aren't you?" He didn't wait for her reply. "Lainie talks about you all the time." He frowned, as if aware that he'd used present tense for somebody whose words would now forever be past tense. "Did you just get in from Chicago?" he asked.

"No, I've been here since Tuesday. I've been staying with my mother since then."

He took a step back from her. "Look, if you'll give me just a minute or two, I'll finish up and get out of your hair."

Before she could reply, he turned and disappeared back into the bathroom. Melody stared at the air where he'd stood, trying to decide if she felt threatened by his presence in the town house or not. She decided she didn't, at least not for the moment, and sank down on the sofa.

Over the past four days, since the police had shown up at the school where she taught in Chicago to tell her that her sister had been murdered, her life had taken on a bizarre quality that hadn't ended. The fact that an unfamiliar, attractive man was scrubbing her sister's bathroom floor was as crazy as it got.

The sheriff had called her mother that morning to let her know he was releasing the condo and that the investigation into Lainie's death had so far yielded no substantive clues.

Melody wasn't surprised. Sheriff Jim Ramsey was a lazy, judgmental man who had probably decided that the investigation into Lainie's death wasn't worth any real effort. Melody hadn't even bothered checking in with him when she'd arrived in town.

What she knew about her sister's murder she'd learned from her mother. Rita Thompson had told Melody that Lainie had been killed in her bathroom sometime between the hours of eleven at night and two in the morning.

There had been no signs of forced entry and she'd been beaten to death with an unknown object. A maid who came in once a week had found her body. Nothing had been stolen, so robbery had been ruled out as a motive.

If I'd just answered the phone, Melody thought. The evening of the murder, Lainie had called Melody. But

Melody had been tired, not in the mood to talk, so she'd let her answering machine pick up the call.

She couldn't help but think that if she'd just answered her phone, the events of that horrible night might have turned out differently. She closed her eyes and the sound of Lainie's message played in her head.

"Hi, sis. Just wanted to check in. Are you there? Well, anyway, I'm really excited. I've got a date with a new guy tonight and who knows, he might just be the one." Lainie had sounded upbeat and happy, and how Melody wished she'd answered that call. She hadn't known that it would be the last time she'd hear her sister's voice.

She jumped to her feet as Hank came back into the room, an empty pail in his hand and the scent of pine cleaner in the air. "I think I got up all the fingerprint dust and everything else," he finished with a touch of awkwardness.

"You didn't have to do that for us," she said. Yet, as she thought of the horrible task he'd just completed, a wave of gratefulness swept over her.

"I did it for Lainie. She wouldn't have wanted you to have to face that." He walked toward the door. "I guess I'll see you this afternoon at the funeral." His blue eyes darkened. "I'm sorry for your loss."

The words should have sounded like the empty platitude spoken at funerals by sympathetic strangers or distant relatives. But, as he spoke, his startling blue eyes filled with darkness and she sensed the true emotion behind the words. He didn't wait for her to reply. With a small nod of his head, he walked out.

She closed the door after him and locked it, then once again slumped on the sofa. She still hadn't processed that her wild, crazy older sister was truly gone.

The real grief had yet to strike, but the guilt that gripped her was nearly paralyzing. She closed her eyes and leaned her head back, remembering the last time she'd seen her sister.

"Don't go," Lainie had said, her lower lip in the infamous pout that had so often gotten her whatever she wanted.

The two were in Melody's bedroom at their mother's home, where Melody had spent most of the day packing up boxes to take with her to Chicago. "I have to go," Melody had replied. "It's a great opportunity and there aren't any teaching jobs available here in Cotter Creek right now."

"You just want to get away from me," Lainie had exclaimed. She'd scooted across the bed and grabbed Melody's hand. "I know you're tired of cleaning up my messes. I know that I'm an emotional vampire, but I promise I'll do better. I swear I'm going to get it together. Melody, what am I going to do when night falls and I get scared? You can't go."

But Melody had left, and now somebody had murdered Lainie. And she couldn't help but feel that if she hadn't left town her sister would still be alive.

She swallowed against the thick emotion that was like a granite weight in her chest. Glancing at her wristwatch, she realized that the funeral was a mere two hours away.

Wearily, she pulled herself up from the sofa. Lainie

had bought the town house five months ago, finally moving out of their mother's home where she'd lived on and off again whenever she was between boyfriends. This building had originally been an old five-story apartment building that had been updated and renovated into town homes for sale.

Lainie had been proud to be a homeowner, although twice in the last four months Melody had sent her sister money to help pay the mortgage and Melody suspected her mother had made at least that many payments and helped with utilities. Lainie had gone through money like she'd gone through men.

The living room was a reflection of Lainie's personality, an explosion of colors and whimsical knickknacks that had probably all been impulse buys. Melody frowned slightly as she gazed at one wall where wild, crazy flowers had been hand-painted. The wall would have to be repainted before the condo was put up for resale.

The slightly chaotic flavor of the living room spilled into the master bedroom, so evocative of Lainie that it brought tears to Melody's eyes.

The spare bedroom held only a bare double bed and a dresser. It was here that Melody placed her suitcase. It took her just minutes to make up the bed with clean linens she found in the hall closet.

After making the bed she hung the clothes from her suitcase, put her nightclothes and underwear in a dresser drawer and her toiletries on top of the dresser.

Her mother had been appalled when Melody had announced her intention to stay in the condo. Her mother saw it as nothing but a place of death, but to Melody it was also the place filled with Lainie's life.

Besides, she'd been sleeping on the sofa at her mother's place. All the spare bedrooms were taken up with relatives who'd come into town for the funeral. It might have seemed morbid to some people, but Melody just felt like she needed to be here.

She had to pack up Lainie's things and get the place ready to put back on the market—and she was hoping that someplace within these walls would be the answer to who might have killed Lainie and why.

And that was the other reason Melody wanted to stay there. Her mother would be upset if she knew Melody intended to do a little investigating on her own.

To most of the people in the small town of Cotter Creek, Lainie had been a throwaway, a wild, bad girl whom everyone expected to come to a bad end.

But to Melody, Lainie had been the sister who had taught her how to laugh, who had introduced her to a world that others didn't see. Lainie had been five years older than Melody, but she'd had the exuberance of a child and a child's fear of the dark. She'd been incredibly dependent on Melody for as long as Melody could remember. The roles of older sister/younger sister had been reversed long ago.

Yes, Lainie had made bad choices. She'd been impulsive and immature, but she'd also been loving and bright and hadn't deserved to die at the young age of thirty.

Melody had spent most of her life taking care of her sister and she wasn't about to stop now. Instinctively she knew that the powers that be in this small town wouldn't knock themselves out to solve the murder of a woman like Lainie. But she would.

She thought of the handsome man who had cleaned up the bathroom and she wondered how close her sister had been to him. Had they been in love? Was he aching with her loss as much as Melody was?

She walked into the kitchen and sat down at the table. This room looked the least used in the place, which wasn't surprising since Lainie had never been much of a cook.

If Melody intended to stay, she needed to buy groceries and see what kind of cooking utensils Lainie had owned. Sure, it would have been much easier to just camp out at her mother's, but that wouldn't do.

Melody needed to be here. School was out for the summer and she didn't have to be back in Chicago for two months. She would use that time to immerse herself in Lainie's surroundings and hopefully ferret out a killer.

Hank gazed around at the people attending Lainie's funeral, surprised at who was missing and also surprised by some of those who had shown up.

He knew Lainie had been seeing a man named Dean, a tough guy who rode a motorcycle and worked as a mechanic down at Hall's Car Haven. Dean was absent from the solemn ceremony, as were all the men Lainie had dated over the last four months of her life.

Grace and Mabel Talbot stood side by side, their gray heads close together as they whispered to each other. The two widowed sisters were responsible for most of the gossip that made the rounds in Cotter Creek. They gave *slander* a new meaning as they chewed up and spit out anyone who didn't live up to their particular moral standards.

Hank stood beneath the shade of an old oak tree and gazed across the flower-laden closed casket to where Lainie's mother, Rita, leaned weakly against Fred Morrison, the man who had been her companion for years.

They made an attractive couple. Even with grief etched deep into her features, Rita was a pretty older woman. Fred, clad in a black suit and carrying his ever-present silver cane, held her tightly.

But it was the woman standing slightly apart from them who captured Hank's attention. Melody looked so alone in her grief.

She wasn't as striking as her sister had been, but there was a quiet beauty in her delicate features. Her dark hair was pulled back at the nape of her neck and her blue eyes were without tears but filled with the kind of pain Hank knew only too well. He was well acquainted with loss and the kind of pain that was so deep it went beyond tears.

Once again he gazed around. He'd heard that killers often attended the funerals of their victims, but he saw nobody he'd believe capable of the violent rage that had propelled Lainie's killer.

The ceremony was blessedly brief and when it was over, Melody walked over to Hank. "Thank you for coming," she said.

"I told you, Lainie was a good friend of mine. I'm going to miss her." His sense of loss at Lainie's death was nothing compared to that of his daughter, Maddie, who had positively adored Lainie.

"Some of us are going to my mother's house. You're welcome to join us there." Her lower lip trembled slightly and the impulse struck him to reach out and take her in his arms, offer her comfort. It shocked him, for it had been a very long time since he'd wanted to take a woman in his arms for any reason.

He glanced at his wristwatch, even though he had nothing to do, nowhere to be. "Thanks, maybe I'll stop by for a little while."

Melody looked at him for a long moment, her thickly fringed blue eyes holding open curiosity. "You've told me you were close to Lainie. I'd like to speak with you about her later…in the next day or two."

If she was looking for answers about the tragedy of Lainie's death, he had few to give her. But he knew about the need to speak of the dead, something many people just didn't understand.

"Anytime." He flashed her a quick smile. "You know where to find me." She nodded and hurried after her mother and Fred, who were walking toward his car.

It took only minutes to reach the Thompson house, where a number of cars were already parked and several people were milling around on the front porch.

When he entered the house, the first person he saw was Melody, who was standing next to her mother and Fred to greet people as they came through the door.

Hank had met both Rita and Fred before. Once when he and Lainie had met them for lunch at a restaurant and then another time when Lainie's car had broken down and Hank had driven her here.

"Hank, thank you for coming." Rita reached for his

hands and squeezed them tightly. "I'm not sure how to live without worrying about Lainie." A choking sob escaped her as she dropped Hank's hands.

Fred, leaning heavily on his cane, reached out and placed an arm around Rita's shoulder. "She's at peace now, honey," he said. "You have to know that Lainie is finally at peace."

Rita nodded and for a moment an awkward silence prevailed. "How about a tall glass of iced tea?" Melody said to Hank, breaking the silence.

"That sounds great," he agreed. He followed her through the living room and into the country kitchen where the table was laden with food.

"Help yourself to anything you want," Melody said, gesturing toward the table.

He watched as she opened the refrigerator and took out a pitcher of iced tea. The scent of her eddied in the air, a floral fragrance he found incredibly attractive. The black-and-white dress she wore emphasized her slender waist and the thrust of her breasts. Her legs were shapely, and a sudden stab of desire struck him.

The time and place was inappropriate for such a feeling but even more shocking was that he felt it at all. Maybe his sorrow at losing Lainie had somehow manufactured some crazy feelings for her sister.

The last thing he wanted was to feel desire for any woman. At least Melody was relatively safe. She'd be out of town before he knew it, back to her own life in Chicago.

He took the glass she held out to him. "Where are you from, Hank?" she asked. "I don't remember seeing you around town before I moved to Chicago."

"Actually, I'm originally from Cotter Creek. Lainie and I were in the same grade from kindergarten to seventh grade. Then my parents moved to Texas. My mom moved back after my dad died."

"I think I remember your family. What brought you back here?" she asked.

"I'm a single parent. I have an eight-year-old daughter, Maddie. About four months ago I decided to make a change. Since Mom lives here now, it seemed a logical place to land. Mom has one of the town houses on the second floor." He broke off, realizing he'd given her far more information than she'd asked for or probably wanted.

"The night Lainie was murdered, you didn't hear anything?" The intensity of her eyes was heartbreaking.

"I'm sorry. I didn't. I'm an early-to-bed, early-to-rise kind of guy, and even though our places share a common wall, the units are fairly soundproof. I wish I had heard something," he said as a wealth of emotion surged up. His hands made tight fists at his sides. "I would have gone inside and stopped it all from happening."

She reached out and placed a hand on his forearm, her fingers hot, as if she were suffering from a fever. "Don't blame yourself." She instantly dropped her hand and took a step backward, her forehead wrinkling with a frown.

"I can't imagine life without her. She was such a big part of my life." She released a small laugh. "Even when I was in Chicago, Lainie managed to fill my life. She'd call at least once a day. Sometimes it was first thing in the morning and other times in the middle of the night."

She shook her head ruefully, a hollowness taking up residency in her eyes. "The night of her murder, she called and I didn't pick up the phone." Her voice dropped to a mere whisper. "I was tired and I just didn't want to deal with any drama, so I let my machine take the call."

He set his glass on the counter, searching his mind for the right thing to say. She hadn't shed a tear during the funeral service but, when her lower lip began to tremble uncontrollably and her blue eyes washed with impending tears, he realized she was now about to lose it.

Hank shifted from one foot to the other, unsure what to do as she seemed to crumble within herself. He didn't know whether he reached for her or she reached for him, but she was suddenly in his arms, sobbing against his chest.

Hank froze for a moment, but as she continued to cry, he wound his arms around her slender back and held her close.

It didn't matter that they were virtually strangers. At the moment they were merely two people mourning a loss. As he held her, he tried not to notice how well she fit into his arms, how the top of her head fit neatly beneath his chin and the press of her breasts was warm and inviting.

What a time for his hormones to kick back to life after being dormant for so long. He wasn't sure what it was about Melody Thompson, but from the moment he'd seen her a spark had gone off inside him—a spark he hadn't felt in years and one he wasn't eager to welcome back.

She cried for only a minute or two longer, then stepped back from him. "I'm sorry." She swiped the tears from her cheeks. "I normally don't fall apart like that."

"Please, don't apologize," he replied. She grabbed a

paper napkin from the table and finished wiping her tears. He stood by awkwardly and waited for her to pull herself together. He picked up his drink from the counter, even though he wasn't thirsty.

"What are your plans now?" he asked.

She tossed the napkin in a nearby trash can, then shrugged. "I have to decide what needs to be done with Lainie's things, then get the town house on the market."

"If there's anything I can do to help, just let me know," he offered.

She smiled then, the first smile he'd seen from her, and pleasure washed over him at the beauty of her expression. "Thanks." The smile fell away and she held his gaze intently. "The most important thing I want to do is find out who killed my sister, and I'm not leaving town until I have an answer."

Chapter 2

Melody grabbed her coffee cup and took another sip. Maybe after two or three cups she'd start feeling alive. She sat at the kitchen table listing everything that needed to be done.

She had three lists started. One detailed what needed to be done to get the place ready for resale. The second had notes she'd made about what to do with Lainie's personal items and the last one simply had the word *Investigation* across the top.

It was just after eight and the morning sun was pouring in through the window, warming her back as she worked. She'd been up far too late the night before, searching Lainie's bedroom for a diary, a notepad, anything that might yield a clue as to whom she'd had a date with on the night of her death.

She'd found nothing. If anything had once been there, then the sheriff and his men had probably removed it when they'd searched the place as a crime scene.

It had been after two when she'd finally fallen into bed, exhausted both mentally and physically. She took another sip of her coffee and stared down at the sheet of paper headed Investigation.

There had been no sign of forced entry. That meant that Lainie knew her attacker, that she'd either opened the door to him or he'd had a key.

Hank Tyler had a key. He'd used it to come in and clean up the blood. And any incriminating evidence he feared might remain? She found it hard to believe that the handsome man who had held her while she wept after the funeral was also a cold-blooded killer.

However, she also knew that to trust anyone right now would be foolish. Just because Hank Tyler was easy on the eyes and seemed to have compassion didn't mean that he wasn't a viable suspect.

There hadn't been anything missing. Whoever had come in hadn't been bent on robbing the place. That meant he'd entered with the specific purpose of harming Lainie.

She picked up her cup once again but, before she could bring it to her lips, she froze. Had she just heard a door open? Her heartbeat quickened, and she thought she heard a furtive movement in the living room.

Had the killer come back?

Sliding out of her seat at the table, she fought the icy chill of fear that threatened to overwhelm her. As quietly as possible, she moved to the drawer that she knew held the knives and grabbed one in her hand.

If she was wrong and nobody was in the condo, then she would chalk it up to an overactive imagination. But if somebody were in the next room, she wouldn't go in unarmed.

Gripping the knife tightly in her fist, she eased out of the kitchen and into the living room to see a dark-haired, blue-eyed little girl sitting on the sofa.

She swallowed a gasp of surprise and dropped the hand that held the knife to her side. "You must be Maddie," she said, remembering that Hank had mentioned his daughter.

The little girl nodded, eyeing Melody as if measuring her worth. "My real name is Madeline Renee Tyler. My friends call me Maddie, but I think you should call me Madeline 'cause I don't know if we're going to be friends or not." She paused a moment. "You aren't as pretty as Lainie."

Melody nodded and surreptitiously placed the knife on one of the end tables. "Lainie was beautiful."

Maddie frowned, her gaze not leaving Melody. "I loved Lainie, but I'm not sure I'm even gonna like you."

An unexpected burst of laughter welled up inside Melody at the little girl's brutal honesty. She managed to swallow it. "I'm not at all sure I'll like you, either."

"You have to like me." Maddie lifted her chin a notch. "It's not polite for grown-ups to dislike little girls."

Again laughter bubbled to Melody's lips. "Maybe when we get to know each other a little better we'll discover that we like each other very much."

Maddie looked at her dubiously. "Do you like chocolate?"

"I love chocolate." Melody sat on the opposite end of the sofa.

"Well then, that's a start," Maddie replied in a voice very grown-up for her age.

"Does your father know you're here?" Melody asked.

"He was in the shower and I was supposed to be watching cartoons, but I decided I wanted to come and meet you. He won't miss me. Lainie used to let me drink soda in the morning." She cast Melody a glance that indicated that this might just be a tiny fib.

"Really? That's strange. Lainie always liked a tall glass of orange juice first thing in the morning," Melody replied. Maddie offered her a sly grin, as if she knew she'd been caught. "Maybe we should call your father and let him know you're here?"

"He'll know as soon as he sees that I'm gone. Whenever I disappear he always knows I'm here or at Grandma's. Besides, I'm mad at him."

Before Melody could ask why the little girl was mad at her daddy, she heard a rapid knock on the door.

Melody got up and opened the door to see Hank. "Hi, is my…" He gazed over her shoulder and spied his daughter. "I'm so sorry," he said to Melody.

"It's all right. Come on in, we were just getting to know each other."

Hank swept past Melody, bringing with him the scent of minty soap and shaving cream. Clad in a pair of navy slacks and a crisp white shirt, he looked in control and amazingly handsome, but definitely irritated with his daughter.

"Give me the key," he said as he stood in front of Maddie.

Her chin thrust out and she grabbed the key that Melody now saw hanging on a chain around her neck. "But Lainie gave it to me," she protested, a hint of moisture shining in her eyes.

"I know, sweetie." Hank crouched down in front of her. "But Lainie isn't here anymore and Melody is going to sell this place to somebody else, so you can't have a key anymore."

Maddie stood up, removed the chain from her neck and handed it to her father as tears filled her eyes. "Why did she have to die?" She glared at Melody. "I don't want you here. I want Lainie." She burst into tears and ran for the door.

"Maddie!" Hank turned to Melody, apology written all over his face. "I'm so sorry."

Melody held up a hand. "Please, don't apologize."

He headed for the door. "Look, she has a birthday party to attend later today. You said you wanted to talk to me about your sister. Would two this afternoon work for you?"

"Okay," she replied.

With another apologetic glance, he hurried after his daughter, and at that moment the phone rang. Melody reached across to the end table and picked up the cordless.

"Have you come to your senses yet? Are you ready to come back here and stay?" Rita said without preamble.

"I never lost my senses, and no, Mom, I'm not ready to come back there. How are you doing this morning?"

"A little better, I think. All the relatives have gone and Fred wanted me to ask you if you're joining us for lunch. He thought it would be nice for me to get out of the house and he's offered to take us to Raymond's. They have wonderful steaks there."

"Thanks, but I'm going to pass," Melody replied. "I want to start boxing up some of the things here." And she didn't want to miss the opportunity to talk with Hank. She needed to find out if he knew who her sister had been seeing, who might have had a motive to want her dead.

"It shouldn't take you too long to get things done there. You need to get back to your own life in Chicago," Rita said. "I'll feel better knowing that you're building your own life. Melody, honey, you gave enough to Lainie."

Yes, she'd given a lot to Lainie, but when her sister had needed her most, she'd been too tired to pick up the phone. "I'll get back to my life when it's time, Mom. Don't worry about me." She decided now wasn't the time to tell her mother that she had no intention of going back to her own life until she found out who had taken her sister's life.

"I've never had to worry about you, Melody. You've always been wonderfully self-sufficient. And you were always so good with Lainie, much better than I was."

It was true. Rita had been at a loss when it came to her eldest daughter. She'd done what she could for Lainie, but usually fell apart at the first sign of trouble. Fred had comforted Rita while most often it had been Melody who stepped in to clean up whatever mess Lainie had made.

There would be no more messes, no more scandals, at least none that involved Lainie because she was gone forever. A feeling of loss nearly took Melody's breath away.

She and her mother small-talked for a few more minutes, then after Melody had promised to have lunch with her mother the next day, they hung up.

Melody wandered back into the kitchen and poured herself a fresh cup of coffee, then sat down and stared at the lists in front of her.

She'd spend the time between now and when Hank arrived packing up Lainie's clothes. Even though the two sisters had been close in size, they couldn't be further apart in styles. Lainie had been flamboyant and Melody much more staid. Melody would donate Lainie's clothes to a local charity.

She'd also donate the furniture. She had no use for it, nor did her mother. There was no point in paying to have it stored.

There were a few personal items she'd keep, like the Guardian Angel picture that had always hung on the wall opposite Lainie's bed and a collection of fairy figurines that had been collected over the years. The fairies had been Lainie's favorite possession and Melody couldn't imagine anyone appreciating them as she would.

She turned her attention to the list that had been on her mind every moment since she'd arrived in town. Staring at the word *Investigation* that she'd written across the top of the page, she wished she would have listened more carefully to Lainie's phone calls in recent weeks.

Most of the time when Lainie called it had been late and Melody had been tired. She'd often listened to her sister's stream-of-consciousness chatter with only half an ear.

She wished she could go back a week or two and

really listen to what Lainie had been saying, listen to whom she'd been seeing and where she'd been going. Somewhere in those conversations there might have been a clue to the killer's identity.

Drawing a deep sigh, she started a final list and at the top of the sheet of paper she wrote the word *Suspects*. She needed to stop by the bar where Lainie had worked as a bartender off and on for the past five years. Maybe one of the waitresses or some of the customers would know whom she'd been seeing at the time of her death.

She took a sip of her coffee, her thoughts lingering on one particular man. She'd been charmed by Hank's daughter. Maddie was outspoken and obviously sharp as a knife—and her grief over Lainie's death had been heartbreaking.

And Hank Tyler had all the characteristics of a heartbreaker. Handsome as sin with an underlying simmering energy and—at least on the surface—a sensitive man. Under different circumstances she might have been interested in him.

But Melody had one rule in life. She never dated men who had dated her sister. She now had a new rule to add to the first. She didn't date men who were potential murder suspects.

She stared at the list titled Suspects and added the first name. Hank Tyler.

Hank knocked on Lainie's door at precisely two o'clock. Melody answered with her purse slung over her shoulder and her car keys in her hand.

"I thought we could talk over coffee out," she said and stepped out of the town house. She firmly pulled the door shut behind her.

"Okay," he said with a touch of surprise. "Anyplace in particular you want to go?"

"Is the café still there on Main Street?" she asked.

"Yeah, it's still there." There was only one.

She nodded. "Then if you don't mind, we'll go there."

He shrugged. "All right by me. It would probably be best if I take my own car because I need to pick up Maddie from the birthday party in two hours."

Hank followed Melody's rental car to the popular café. While he was driving, he realized the reason she'd wanted to speak with him out in public. She thought he might be Lainie's killer.

And why wouldn't she regard him with suspicion? Somebody Lainie knew, somebody she had either let into her condo or who had used a key to enter, had killed her. Melody knew he had a key and he'd told her he'd been close to Lainie. She'd be a fool not to suspect him.

Maybe over coffee he could convince her that he had no reason to kill Lainie, that it had been Lainie who had brought laughter back to his life after it had been missing for too long.

Even though the lunch rush was over, there were few empty tables and booths in the café, which was a popular place for women to share tea and retired men to sip coffee and pass the time.

As he walked in the door, he spied Melody already seated at a booth in the back. The coral blouse she wore brought out the color in her cheeks and made her eyes appear impossibly blue.

He headed toward the booth and couldn't help but remember how she'd felt in his arms the day before, so warm and for just a moment so yielding.

He mentally shoved the image away as he slid into the seat opposite her. He'd just settled in when the waitress arrived to take their order.

"Coffee," Melody said.

"Make it two, and I'll take a piece of apple pie," Hank said to the waitress, then smiled at Melody. "Sure you don't want a piece of pie or something?"

She shook her head. "No, thanks. I just had lunch a little while ago."

The waitress left and she pulled a small notepad and pen from her purse and set them on the table before her. He eyed them curiously. "I feel like I'm about to be deposed by a lawyer."

A tinge of red danced into her cheeks. "For the last couple of days I've been so frazzled, I think it's important I take notes so I won't forget anything you say."

"I'm not sure what it is you want from me," he replied.

The waitress arrived at their table and served their coffee and his pie. When the waitress left, Melody wrapped her fingers around her cup as if seeking warmth to chase away some inner chill.

"Lainie and I had kind of an unspoken agreement. Even though she told me when she was going out with somebody, she didn't give me all the details. She knew I disapproved of her dating habits." Melody laughed suddenly, a short but musical burst she instantly stifled.

"I sound like a prude and I'm not, but I knew Lainie was promiscuous." She said the last word with a wince, as if it hurt coming out of her mouth.

Hank knew he had two choices. He could either protest her assessment of her sister or he could be completely truthful. He opted for truth. "Lainie was obviously looking for something she couldn't find."

"Lainie was mentally ill." Again there was a wealth of pain lacing her words. "She was never officially diagnosed with anything, refused to see a doctor. But I truly believe she was bipolar or something like that."

"We talked about that," he said. She looked at him in surprise. "Lainie knew she was out of sync with the world, but she was afraid of taking medication, of somehow losing herself to drugs in an effort to be normal."

Melody stared at him for a long moment, her blue eyes thoughtful. "You must have been very close to her."

"I didn't kill her, Melody." He leaned forward slightly, wanting to take away any doubt that might linger in her head. "I had no reason to kill your sister. You saw how my daughter loved Lainie. Aside from the fact that I'm not capable of beating a woman to death, I'd never hurt my daughter by harming somebody she loved. She's had enough loss in her life. I cared about Lainie. She was like a little sister to me."

There was no way to explain to her that when he'd arrived in Cotter Creek he'd still been deep in a grieving process that had lasted for far too long. It had been Lainie's irrepressible sense of humor and warmth that had chipped away at the emotional shell he'd built around himself.

Instead of taking away the faint frown that stretched across her forehead, his words deepened it. "You weren't her lover?"

"Never." He leaned back against the booth. "Lainie had plenty of lovers. What she needed was a good friend, and that's what I tried to be to her." And that's what he'd needed in his life as well.

She picked up her coffee and took a sip, her gaze not wavering from his. He felt as if he were on trial and the jury was still out.

She placed her cup back on the table, then picked up her pen. "Do you know the names of some of the men Lainie had been seeing just before that night?"

That night. It was as if she found it impossible to say the word *killed* or *murdered.* "I know she was off and on with a man named Dean Lucas. He's a mechanic. Works at Hall's Car Haven." He watched as she wrote the information down on her pad. Her long dark hair fell forward, looking shiny and soft, and he was surprised by his impulse to reach out and touch it.

Throughout his relationship with Lainie, he'd learned a lot about Melody Thompson. He knew she had just turned twenty-six, that she'd been the one person Lainie had depended on and that, according to Lainie, Melody had never had a serious romantic relationship.

He found the last hard to believe. She was gorgeous, and bright, with an underlying sensuality that was more than a little appealing. Not that he was interested. When he'd buried his wife, he'd made a vow that there would be no other woman in his life on a permanent basis…ever.

"Who else?" she asked, pulling him from his thoughts.

"She had problems with a guy named James O'Donnell a couple of months ago. I don't think they were dating, but she thought he was obsessed with her. I think Lainie called the cops on him because she thought he was stalking her."

She wrote down that information as well, then took another sip of her coffee. "You'd better eat your pie before it gets cold."

He picked up his fork and cut into the pie, but the last thing on his mind was food. "Why do you want that information? I've already told the sheriff everything I know."

"Sheriff Ramsey is an idiot who couldn't find a criminal if one came up and introduced himself," she exclaimed, her voice rich with derision.

"Ramsey isn't the sheriff anymore," Hank replied. "Zack West is sheriff now."

She raised one of her dark, perfectly arched brows. "Really? I didn't know. I haven't talked to anyone but family members since I've been back in town."

For a moment they were silent. He ate his pie and she stared down at the short list of names he'd given her.

Lainie had been incredibly easy to read. She'd worn her emotions on her face where everyone could see them. Melody gave away little of what she was thinking or feeling. It was an easy guess that she was a far more complicated woman than her sister had been.

"Your daughter is a little charmer," she said, finally breaking the silence that had grown between them.

"She's far too smart and too outspoken for her own good. Which reminds me…" He dug into his pocket and pulled out two keys. "Here are the keys that Lainie gave us to her apartment." He placed them on the table between them. "I don't know who else she might have given a key to, so it might be a good idea to change the locks."

She nodded. "I'll have somebody come out first thing in the morning. Is there anything else you can tell me about what was going on with Lainie around the time of her death? Anything unusual?"

He hesitated a long moment, unsure about revealing the confidences of a woman now dead. "What?" she asked as she leaned forward.

"Did you know she wanted a baby? That she was trying to get pregnant?" He could tell by the shocked look on her face that Lainie hadn't shared that with her.

A spasm of grief twisted her features and he bit his tongue, sorry that he'd told her. "That's the last thing she needed. She couldn't even take care of herself, let alone a baby," she said.

"I'm sorry, I shouldn't have told you," he said, fighting the impulse to reach out and take her hand, offer some sort of physical support. She looked so sad, so lost.

"No, I want you to tell me everything. If I'm going to find the person who killed her then I need to know everything."

He stared at her in surprise. "Don't you think it would be best to leave the investigation to the sheriff and his men?"

She leaned back, looking stronger than she had moments before. "I'll let the sheriff run his investigation but I intend to run my own. If I know my sister, she liked to run with people who had at least as many problems as she did, people with attitudes and criminal records, not the kind of people who will likely cooperate with anyone in law enforcement. They'll talk to me."

Hank thought about the blood he'd cleaned up. So much blood. Whoever had killed Lainie had been enraged. The violence that had taken place in that bathroom sickened him.

He wanted to talk Melody out of whatever it was she intended to do, but he could tell by the fervent glow in her eyes that she was determined.

"That could be dangerous. Do you have a plan?" he asked.

"The first place I'm going to start asking questions is at the Edge," she replied. "Maybe Lainie's boss or one of her coworkers will know something."

Hank scowled. "That bar is no place for a woman to go by herself. Why don't I tag along with you?"

"I can't ask you to do that," she replied.

"You didn't ask. I offered."

Once again she stared at him for a long moment. He'd thought her eyes were a clear, sharp blue like Lainie's, but he realized now they were deeper, darker and far more enigmatic than her sister's.

"I was planning on going tonight," she finally said.

He nodded. "Maddie can stay at my mother's."

"How do I know I can trust you?" she asked. Some of the fervor left her eyes and she suddenly looked small and vulnerable.

"You know any of the West family?" he asked.

"I know them on sight and by reputation. I know they work in the bodyguard business. Why?"

"Dalton West is an old friend of mine. One of the reasons I decided to make the move from Texas to Cotter Creek was so I could go to work for them. At the moment I'm waiting to be assigned to my first job with them."

Maybe four months of boredom was getting to him, or maybe he was jumping into her drama because he had genuinely grown to care for Lainie. "Maybe we could help each other," he continued. "It sounds to me like you intend to talk to people and go places that might put a single, attractive woman at risk. You could use a bodyguard, and I could use some practice at being a bodyguard."

"So, you want to be my bodyguard in training?" A small smile curved her lips.

He returned her smile. "Something like that."

Once again she wrapped her fingers around her coffee cup and eyed him soberly. "I'll think about it," she said finally.

He nodded and told himself it really didn't matter to him whether she took his offer of help or not. Eventually the killer would be caught and Melody Thompson would return to her life in Chicago.

And he'd keep putting one foot in front of the other and try to figure out how to keep going when the only woman he'd ever loved was gone.

Chapter 3

Melody stared at her reflection in the bedroom mirror. She scarcely recognized the woman who looked back at her. Tight jeans molded to her and the bright turquoise blouse fit her like a second skin, the plunging neckline revealing far more flesh than she was used to showing.

If she was going to hang out at the Edge, then it was important for her to blend in with the clientele that frequented the bar on the edge of town. Her conservative clothes would set her apart, draw attention that she didn't want, so she'd raided Lainie's closet for something appropriate.

Her hand trembled slightly as she raised it to smooth an errant strand of hair away from her face. She knew that she might be asking questions tonight that could make somebody nervous.

She turned away from the mirror and checked her wristwatch. Almost nine. Hank would be here soon to accompany her to the bar.

She wasn't sure why she trusted Hank Tyler, but she did. There was something solid about him. She liked his direct gaze and the straight answers he'd given her over coffee. Besides, he was working for the West family. That went a long way in alleviating any fear she might have that he was a nut.

After she'd left the café and Hank that afternoon, she'd gone straight to the sheriff's office and met with Zack West. He'd assured her that they were doing everything in their power to find Lainie's killer.

"But I'll be straight with you, Melody. We don't have any real leads and your sister didn't have a conventional lifestyle."

"The night of the murder she left a message on my answering machine and told me she was going out with somebody new. I don't suppose you've identified who that might have been?" she'd asked.

Zack shook his head, his green eyes sympathetic. "Not yet. But I've told your mother and I'm telling you, I won't rest until we have the killer behind bars."

She'd left the office satisfied that Zack and his men were doing everything they could to solve the crime, but unsure just how successful they would be.

As irrational as it was, she felt as if she were the only one who could find the answers. She was the one who had known Lainie better than anyone and she owed it to her sister to help her rest in peace. The only way that would happen was if Lainie's murderer was found and punished.

The soft knock on her door pulled her from her thoughts and she hurried to answer. Hank had under-dressed for the night as well. Clad in tight worn jeans and a black T-shirt that stretched across his broad shoulders, he looked both slightly dangerous and capable of handling anything that might come his way.

"Are you sure you want to do this?" he asked as she grabbed her purse from the sofa.

"Are you sure you want to?" she countered.

He flashed her a small smile. "I'm in if you are."

"Then let's go." She locked the door behind her and together they left the building and walked out into the warm night air.

"We'll take my car," he said as he pulled a set of keys from his pocket. "If we run into any problems I know mine has the horsepower we need to make a fast get-away." He gestured toward a bright red sports car, a larger model that seated four.

"Definitely better horsepower than my rental," she agreed. "Are you expecting trouble?"

He shrugged. "I like to be a good Boy Scout and be prepared for anything." He opened the passenger door and she slid inside, then watched as he went around the front of the car to the driver's side.

She drew a tremulous sigh. Hank Tyler had been attractive in his dress slacks and shirt, but he looked like pure sin in those jeans and T-shirt. His dark hair fell care-lessly over his forehead and only added to his lethal look.

"You don't need that kind of distraction," she muttered to herself as he slid in behind the steering wheel.

Fastening her seat belt, she tried to ignore the scent

of him, a pleasant fragrance that reminded her of sunshine and sandalwood. "You must have moved into the town houses right around the time Lainie did," she said, determined to keep her focus on the matter at hand.

He started the engine with a roar and pulled out onto the street. "She moved in a couple of weeks before me and Maddie. The first night we were there she brought over a little basket of soaps she'd collected from hotel rooms over the years." He smiled. "She said she didn't have any fruit and refused to bake a cake, but wanted to welcome us and bring us something. Maddie still uses the soaps. She says they're just her size."

A new edge of grief crawled up in the back of Melody's throat as she thought of her sister. "Lainie loved hotel soap and shampoo. When any of us stayed at a hotel, we always grabbed the freebies for her."

They cruised slowly down Main Street and Melody looked at him curiously. "Where were you before coming here? You mentioned something about Texas?"

"Just south of Dallas. My grandfather was an Oklahoma oil man, and when he passed away he left me an embarrassingly large inheritance. I used it to buy a ranch. I raised cattle and horses."

"What made you decide to leave it all and come back to Cotter Creek?"

In the illumination from the dashboard she saw his hands tighten slightly on the steering wheel. "My wife died." The words fell flat, with no other information offered.

It was obviously a topic he didn't want to discuss. "I'm sorry," she said.

"Thanks."

They were silent for several minutes. So, he wasn't a stranger to grief, she thought. She realized that's what he'd meant earlier when he'd told her that his daughter had suffered enough loss in her life.

Her heart ached for Maddie, who had lost a mother so early in life. Melody knew what it was like to lose a parent. She'd lost her father when she'd been ten, and while Fred had stepped in as a father figure and support, it would never be the same as having her own dad in her life.

A new tension filled her as Hank turned off the main road and onto a gravel road that led to the Edge. Was she foolish to think that she could get information that Zack West couldn't? Perhaps. All she knew was that she needed to try.

"Looks like a full house," he said as the place came into view. A sprawling one-story building, it was weathered to a dark gray with neon signs in the windows that advertised a variety of beer.

Motorcycles were parked in a row by the front door and the parking lot was filled with pickups and cars. A group of men stood just outside the front door, their cowboy hats pulled low in tough-guy fashion.

Hank found an empty parking space and pulled in, then together they got out of the car. As they approached the door, Hank threw an arm across her shoulder in a proprietary fashion. She welcomed it, was glad that he was with her as the men eyed her up and down with drink-induced boldness.

Hank met their stares with a hint of challenge as

he and Melody passed them to go inside. Anxiety twisted in her stomach as they entered the dim, noisy, smoky tavern.

Hank pointed to two empty stools at the bar and Melody quickly beelined for them. "Two beers," Hank said to the bartender, a young man with tattooed arms and a pierced ear.

"Bottle or tap?"

"Bottle," Melody said. She wasn't sure she wanted to drink from any glass the place had to offer.

The bartender set the beer in front of them and Hank tossed a bill on the counter. "Is Harry in?" She had to yell to be heard above the sound of the band that was playing on a platform stage at the other end of the place.

The bartender glanced at his wristwatch and then shook his head. "He usually shows up around ten or so."

"Can you let me know when he gets here?" she asked.

He nodded and moved down the bar to serve another customer. "Who's Harry?" Hank asked. He leaned so close to her she felt his warm breath on the side of her neck. It danced a shiver of pleasure up her spine.

"Harry Pryor, the owner," she replied. She picked up her beer, then swiveled her stool around to face the crowd. The dance floor was packed with two-stepping cowboys and women dressed to attract Mr. Right, or at least Mr. Right at the Moment.

So many people, she thought. How was she ever going to find the ones who might have been close to Lainie? How could she even begin to try to figure out who might have answers that could lead to a killer?

She looked at Hank, who scanned the crowd with

narrowed, calculating eyes. "See anyone you know?" she asked.

He shook his head. "I was hoping to see either Dean or James here, but I don't see either of them."

"It's early," Melody replied. She turned back around and motioned to the bartender. When he approached them she offered him her brightest smile. "I was just wondering if you were friends with Lainie Thompson."

He grabbed a wet sponge and swiped down the countertop. "Who's asking?"

"I'm Melody Thompson, Lainie's sister."

Immediately his expression changed as a smile exposed a chipped front tooth. "Everyone was Lainie's friend. She used to talk about you a lot." The smile fell. "I can't believe what happened to her."

"You know anyone who was angry with her? Somebody she was fighting with or who was giving her a hard time?" Melody asked.

His gaze shifted to Hank, then back to Melody. "Is he a cop?"

Hank shook his head. "Just a friend."

"I already talked to the sheriff and told him I don't know anyone who was upset with Lainie, unless maybe it was Harry. But Harry was always mad at Lainie. He'd fire her at closing then rehire her the next day. Look, I really don't know anyone who'd want to hurt Lainie." Once again he moved away from them as a customer hollered for him.

Hank leaned closer to Melody. "Anyone else you see that you want to question?"

Once again she gazed around the room and spied a

waitress in black tights, a short skirt and a tight T-shirt that advertised the Edge. "The waitress over there. Her name is Kerry Butcher. She was one of Lainie's friends." She slid off the stool.

"Want me to come with you?" Hank asked.

"No, I'll just see if I can grab her when she brings over her next drink order." Besides, Melody suddenly needed a bit of distance from Hank Tyler. She was finding it difficult to focus on what she was there for with his evocative scent washing over her and his body warming hers.

She'd been cold ever since she'd been told about her sister's murder, and she found Hank's warmth far too appealing for comfort.

She wound her way through the crowd and touched Kerry's arm. The big-breasted, wild-haired woman spun around to face her. Her caramel-colored eyes instantly took on the sheen of tears. "Melody! What are you doing here?"

"I need to talk to you about Lainie," Melody replied.

Kerry frowned as somebody at a nearby table called her name. "I've got a break coming up in about ten minutes. Meet me in the back of the building."

As Melody returned to the bar she couldn't help but notice that Hank was the most attractive man in the place and was garnering plenty of admiring female glances.

Another place, another time, she might have considered following through on her initial attraction to him, but he was merely an emotional support while she navigated her way through her sister's murder investigation. Nothing more.

By summer's end she'd be back in Chicago living the life she'd begun there. There had only been two weeks left of school when she'd gotten the word about Lainie's death and Mr. Cook, the principal at the school, had assured her the job would be waiting for her in the fall.

"Everything okay?" Hank asked as she rejoined him at the bar.

"I'm supposed to meet her behind the building in ten minutes when she takes her break."

"Maybe she'll be able to tell you something you can take to Zack." He frowned. "I know it's really none of my business, but I don't think it's wise for you to be putting yourself out here like this, asking questions that could possibly stir somebody up in a very bad way."

Melody lifted her bottle of beer to her lips and took a swallow, her mouth suddenly unaccountably dry as she felt an unexpected press of tears.

She set the bottle back down on the bar, then leaned closer to Hank. "I just need to do this," she said. "You don't have to help me, but I have to do this, with or without you."

For a long moment his gaze held hers and the noise, the crowd and their entire surroundings fell away as she felt as if he were looking deep inside her and saw her need. He covered her hand with his and smiled. "Body-guards in training don't quit before the job is done."

She smiled at him gratefully. "Thank you."

"And now, let's head out back and see what your waitress friend has to tell us."

* * *

It was almost midnight when Hank and Melody left the Edge with precious little information gained. As they got back into his car he could feel her depression weighing heavily on her.

Kerry hadn't known who Lainie was seeing at the time of her death, although she did mention both Dean and James as men in Lainie's recent past. Harry, the owner of the tavern, had also had little information to give them, except mentioning that Lainie had been talking about wanting to have a baby.

They'd spoken with him in his cramped office in the back of the building, and he'd told them that he didn't remember any customers having problems with Lainie or her talking about having any kind of trouble with anyone else.

"I guess it was silly of me to think I'd just waltz right in and find out all the answers that Zack hasn't been able to find," she said, breaking the silence that had built between them. She released a weary sigh.

"Not silly, just a bit unrealistic," he replied.

"I hope your mother isn't upset that we stayed so late."

"She's keeping Maddie overnight so it's not an issue." He turned into the parking lot of the town houses, surprised to discover that he was sorry the night was about to end.

It had been a long time since anything or anyone had captured his interest. Certainly he was interested in seeing Lainie's murderer brought to justice, but he had to confess that he was quickly becoming equally intrigued by Melody.

When he'd first arrived at Lainie's place that evening, her appearance had punched him right in the gut. She'd looked hot in her tight jeans and turquoise blouse, and throughout the evening he'd hardly been able to keep his eyes off her.

He'd had one brief affair a year ago with a woman he'd known had no expectations of a happily-ever-after. He had a feeling that Melody Thompson wasn't at all like that.

As they'd sat in the bar watching the crowd, the toe-tapping music had made him want to grab Melody in his arms and swing her out on the dance floor. He'd wanted to feel her body pressed against his, move in the rhythm that mimicked sex.

Rebecca had loved to dance. Almost every Friday night she'd asked Hank to go with her to the local honky-tonk for a night of dancing. Most Friday nights he'd declined. He'd been too tired, preferred spending his evenings alone with Rebecca and Maddie rather than in a bar with loud music and drinkers.

When Melody wasn't asking questions about her sister, they'd talked, passing the time and getting to know each other better. She was easy to talk to, both intelligent and quick-witted.

He parked and they got out of the car. "You want to come in for a little while?" she asked when they reached her door. "I know it's late but I'm a little wound up. I could make some coffee."

He smiled. "Coffee is the last thing you need if you're already wound up." He could tell by the soft plea in her eyes that she didn't want to be alone. "But, I would come in for a tall glass of water."

She flashed him a grateful smile and unlocked her door. He followed her through the living room and into the kitchen where he sat at the table while she got out the glasses and ice.

"Thank you for tonight," she said as she placed his glass of water in front of him.

"You don't have to thank me," he replied as she sat in the chair opposite him. "I want Lainie's murderer caught, too."

Melody took a sip of her water, then stared out the window where the blackness of night was profound. "She hated the night," she said softly. "She read a poem when she was younger. I don't know who wrote it or where she found it, but it started out something like… 'When night falls and takes the day, that's when evil comes out to play.' I don't remember the rest of it. She told me once that when night fell and she was alone, she feared she'd disappear. It was her biggest fear and it breaks my heart that it came true."

Melody looked at him, her eyes filled with pain. "As silly as it sounds, I think it would have been easier if she'd been murdered during the day instead of at night when she was most frightened anyway."

Her words broke his heart. Once again he had the desire to pull her into his arms and offer comfort, promise her that the pain would pass and life would go on. But how could he promise her that when he wasn't at all sure it was the truth? It had been two years, and his pain was still as raw as it had been the night that Rebecca slipped from this world.

"Tell me about your life in Chicago," he said, hoping

the change of subject would take away the shadows from her eyes. "Lainie told me you're a teacher."

"Third grade. I love kids that age, around Maddie's age."

"You always wanted to be a teacher?"

"Not always." She leaned back in the chair and for the first time since the evening had begun she looked relaxed. The tiny line of stress that had streaked across her forehead had disappeared and her mouth looked less tense. "For the first two years of college I wasn't sure what I wanted to do with my life."

"You went to Maple Park College?" he asked, knowing the small school was a mere twenty minutes away.

She smiled. "I think almost everyone who lives in Cotter Creek attends Maple Park Community College at one time or another." She took a sip of the water, then continued. "For a long time I thought my job in life was going to be taking care of Lainie. She never wanted me to be too far away from her."

"But you moved to Chicago."

She leaned forward, the line of stress once again creasing her forehead. "By the time I graduated and realized I wanted to teach, there were no jobs here in Cotter Creek. Actually, it was Lainie who initially en-couraged me to take a job wherever I could get one. She was feeling particularly good at the time, strong and in-dependent. So I got the offer from the school in Chicago and decided to take it. I was thrilled when I heard that Lainie had decided to move out of Mom's home and into her own place. But I could tell by her phone calls that she wasn't having an easy time without me." She sighed, as if the long explanation had exhausted her.

"Lainie mentioned you didn't date much. You have somebody special in Chicago?"

She laughed. "Nobody special, nobody even casual. I haven't had time to do much of anything except work and settle into my apartment. I did have one serious relationship when I was in college, but in the end I broke it off. He told me he was tired of Lainie's phone calls interrupting us when we were together and basically gave me a him-or-her choice."

"And blood is thicker than water," he replied.

"In this case, definitely. But that's enough about me. Tell me about you. Did you always want to be a bodyguard?"

"Never entered my mind until about six months ago. I needed a change. I was tired of ranching. My mom lived here and it seemed a logical choice. As far as the bodyguard work, Dalton West is an old friend of mine and he's the one who initially suggested it to me."

"Isn't it dangerous?" she asked.

The only danger he felt at the moment was from the glossy shine of her lips, which seemed to beg for a kiss, and the scent of her fragrance, which eddied in the air and made him want to explore exactly where on her body it came from.

"I served in the military for four years, I'm a crack shot with a gun and I've been trained in hand-to-hand combat. I feel fairly confident that I can handle whatever comes my way," he replied.

He stood, realizing that it was time to go. He was

finding her nearness far too appealing and had a feeling that if he remained she'd ask questions he didn't want to answer. "It's late," he said.

She got up as well. "I've taken up far too much of your time," she said as she walked with him to the front door. "Thank you, Hank, for going with me." She placed a hand on his arm and smiled up at him, and the muscles in his stomach tightened in response.

"What's your next plan?" he asked.

She dropped her hand to her side. "I think sometime tomorrow I'll take my rental car in for an oil change at Car Haven."

"And maybe question Dean Lucas?"

She nodded. "From what you told me he was probably the last guy Lainie was dating."

His impulse was to offer to accompany her, but he knew she'd be okay talking to Dean in broad daylight in public. She didn't need him and he needed some distance. "Then I'll just say good-night."

As he walked out of Lainie's town house he tried to summon up a mental image of his wife, Rebecca, but all he could visualize was how Melody's blouse had given him a tantalizing glimpse of her breasts, how she'd looked at him as if he were her own personal hero all evening.

He didn't want to be her hero, but if he were perfectly honest with himself he'd admit that he wouldn't mind taking her to bed. It had been far too long since he'd had the warmth of a female body in his arms, enjoyed the release that came with making love. And Melody was the first woman in a long time to remind him of that.

But he was certain the last thing on her mind was an uncommitted night of sex. She was focused solely on her goal—to catch a killer—and at the moment his sole focus should be keeping her safe from any trouble her investigation might bring her way.

Chapter 4

"Why on earth would you want to involve yourself in a matter for the sheriff?" Rita asked Melody, her raised voice drawing the attention of other diners in the restaurant. After spending the morning packing away some of the items in the town house, Melody had rushed to meet Fred and her mother for lunch.

Fred placed a hand on Rita's to calm her, but his look at Melody was just as outraged as her mother's. "Melody, Dean Lucas is a hooligan. You have no business having anything to do with that young man."

Melody couldn't believe Fred had actually used the term *hooligan* and she couldn't believe that she'd been stupid enough to tell them that she was doing a little investigating into Lainie's murder on her own.

"I'm just asking a few questions here and there. Don't you both want to know who killed Lainie?"

"Of course we do," Fred blustered. "But that's Zack West's job. He's a good man. He'll eventually find the guilty person."

"Eventually isn't soon enough for me," Melody replied.

"I couldn't bear it if anything happened to you, too," Rita said. She reached over and grabbed Melody's hand and squeezed it tightly. "You don't even need to stay there to pack up the rest of the town house. Fred and I can do it. I just want you safe and happy, not involving yourself in this ugliness."

Melody pulled her hand from her mother's. "I owe Lainie this. It's something I need to do, and stop worrying about me."

"How's the packing coming?" Fred asked, in an obvious ploy to change the subject.

"Slowly, but it's getting done," Melody replied. She twisted her napkin in her lap, wishing she were back at the town house plotting her next move.

"I understand there's a wall in the town house that needs to be painted. You want me to send one of my men over to take care of it?" Fred owned a large construction firm.

Melody looked at him curiously. "You haven't been in the town house before?"

"Not inside," he replied. "Lainie kept telling us she was going to invite us over, but every time we'd bring it up she'd tell us the place wasn't quite ready for company."

"She was trying so hard to be independent," Rita said, her eyes radiating the sadness of a mother's heartbreak. "Fred didn't want to intrude on her privacy."

"Just say the word and I'll get a couple of men in

there to do whatever needs to be done to get it on the market as soon as possible so you can get on with your life," Fred said.

Melody laughed. "I'm beginning to think that the two of you are trying to get rid of me."

"Don't be silly," Rita exclaimed. "You know I love having you here, but I know you've begun a new life in Chicago and there's really nothing here for you."

"And I'm hoping to finally convince your mother to make a new life with me," Fred said. "I've asked her to marry me."

Melody smiled at the man who had been in her mother's life for years. "Fred, you've asked my mother to marry you at least a dozen times before."

He gazed at Rita fondly. "But I think this time she's going to say yes. She's wearing my ring around her neck."

Rita smiled and pulled a chain from beneath her blouse. Hanging on it was Fred's college ring with its blue stone. Melody found it corny, but oddly charming. "I told him I'm willing to go steady, but I'm still thinking about marriage." She smiled coyly.

My mother has a better love life than I do, Melody thought and found that fact incredibly depressing. Her mind instantly filled with a vision of Hank. She'd felt so safe with him the night before, and after they'd gotten back to Lainie's he'd seemed to know that she wasn't ready to be alone.

Her thoughts of Hank suddenly turned unsettling as she wondered what those broad shoulders would feel like naked beneath her fingers. She wondered what those lips of his might taste like in a fiery kiss.

The rest of the lunch was pleasant enough as Fred and her mother talked about a cruise they were taking in the fall and some renovations Fred had decided to do on his home.

After lunch she left the restaurant and headed down Main to Hall's Car Haven. As she drove, her thoughts scattered in a million directions. She hoped her mother finally married Fred. He'd certainly waited for her long enough.

Fred had been partners with Melody's father, James. James had died of a heart attack when Melody was ten and Lainie fifteen. Fred had been a huge support to the grieving widow and eventually their friendship had developed into something deeper.

Melody's thoughts turned to Steve, the young man she'd dated in college. When he'd given her the ultimatum of choosing either Lainie or him, the choice had been remarkably easy and she'd realized at that time that she wasn't in love with him.

Lainie had needed her and since the time they were young, Lainie's need had been enough to fill Melody. Now, with Lainie gone, Melody felt more alone, emptier than she'd ever felt in her life.

Was it any wonder that she was vulnerable to Hank Tyler's charms? Lainie's death had left a huge hole inside her and surely her visceral attraction to Hank was simply the need to fill that hole.

She shook her head to clear her mind as she pulled into Hall's Car Haven, where several cars were on lifts and a small group of men clustered around the front door.

Nerves tightened her stomach muscles as she got out of her car and approached the front door. The men moved aside for her to enter. The minute she walked in and saw the man behind the counter, she knew he was Dean.

His long black hair framed a handsome face that had the lean, slightly dangerous look that had always attracted Lainie. Tattoos covered his arms but he smiled pleasantly at her. "Can I help you?"

"I hope so. Are you Dean?"

His dark eyes narrowed slightly. "Who's asking?"

"I'm Melody Thompson, Lainie's sister."

A flash of pain streaked across his features. "What are you doing here?"

"I was just wondering if I could ask you a few questions."

He looked around, as if wishing that somebody else would come in. He finally looked back at her and drew a deep sigh. "Look, I already told the sheriff I don't know anything about her murder. We broke up a couple of weeks before and I was with my new girlfriend the night Lainie was killed."

"Did you know who she might have gone out with the night she was murdered?"

He shook his head. "After we broke up, we didn't talk anymore."

"Whose idea was it to break up?"

"It was mutual. We were just kicking it, you know. Neither one of us was in love or anything like that. We dated for a couple of weeks and decided it wasn't working. No hard feelings, no big drama."

Disappointment fluttered through her. "So you don't know anyone who might have wanted her dead?"

"Sorry, I can't help you."

"Thanks for your time." She turned to leave but stopped as he called her name.

"You know she wanted a kid. She told me she didn't want to get married or anything like that, but she wanted a baby. That's why we broke up. I'm not ready for kids."

"You know where I can find James O'Donnell?"

His eyes flashed darkly. "Why do you want to find him? He's a crazy dude. That's who I figured killed her, but Sheriff West said he had an alibi for that night."

"I'd still like to talk to him."

"He works most nights at the video store on Main. I don't know where he hangs during the days when he isn't working."

"Thanks, Dean." She turned and left, thinking that he'd been telling the truth. At least she hadn't had to pay for an oil change in order to talk to the man. But that was a small comfort, considering she really hadn't gotten any new information.

She headed home, deciding that she'd spend the rest of the afternoon packing up more of Lainie's things. She'd been home only about thirty minutes when there was a knock at the door.

Maddie marched in when she answered, a bag of chocolate-chip cookies in her hand. "I'm still not sure I'm going to like you, but I thought maybe you'd like to eat some cookies with me," she announced.

"I was just thinking maybe it was time for a cookie break," Melody replied as the two headed for the kitchen table.

Maddie set the bag on the table, then went to the

refrigerator and pulled out the gallon of milk. "My grandma baked these cookies. They were Lainie's favorites. Lainie always said a chocolate-chip cookie could fix almost anything, but no matter how many I eat, I'm still mad at my dad." She scooted into a chair at the table.

"Why are you mad at your dad?" Melody asked as she poured them each a glass of milk, then put the jug back in the refrigerator.

"Just because," Maddie replied as she opened the bag of cookies and took one out. "My mommy's dead."

"I know. My daddy died when I was about your age," Melody replied.

Maddie chewed thoughtfully, her gaze not leaving Melody. "Do you remember your daddy?"

"Not a lot," Melody confessed. "It was a long time ago and I was pretty young."

"Sometimes I don't hardly remember my mom. Grandma says she was perfect for my daddy and that his heart will hurt forever. I wish his heart would stop hurting so he could maybe find me a new mom." She took another bite of her cookie while Melody digested this information about Hank.

Maddie took a drink of her milk and wiped her milk mustache off with the back of her hand. Melody got up and grabbed a paper towel and handed it to her. She murmured a thank-you and reached for another cookie.

"I liked coming here to see Lainie. My grandma always tells me what to do and my daddy hardly talks to me at all, but Lainie always talked to me."

"It's important to have a friend to talk to," Melody replied.

"Which do you like better? Cowboys or bodyguards?"

Melody sat back in her chair at the abrupt change of subject. "I don't know. I've never really thought about it before," she replied, wondering what was going on in the little girl's head.

Beneath the obvious intelligence and touch of bravado Melody suspected there was a hurt little girl who needed something she wasn't getting.

"Aren't you going to eat a cookie?" Maddie asked.

"Absolutely," Melody agreed and grabbed one. "Mmm, your grandma is a good cookie baker," she said after taking a bite.

"Grandma cooks everything good. Lainie couldn't cook. Sometimes she'd order pizza and we'd eat it right out of the box. I love pizza."

A knock sounded at the door and Maddie frowned. "That will be my dad or my grandma." She didn't move from her seat at the table.

"Then I guess I'd better answer it," Melody said as she got up. She opened the door to find Hank, a deep frown cut across his forehead.

"Is my daughter here?"

Maddie appeared in the living room doorway. "Maddie, you've got to stop bothering Melody," he said at the sight of her.

"I'm afraid this is all my fault. She isn't bothering me. I invited her in," Melody said, figuring the little white lie wouldn't hurt. "We were just talking about having a pizza party."

Maddie moved to stand next to Melody, and to her surprise the little girl slipped her hand into Melody's.

"You like pizza, Daddy. You could come to the party, too." There was a faint wistfulness in her words.

Hank looked at his daughter for a long moment, then gazed at Melody. "When and where is this pizza party?"

"Tomorrow night, right here. I'll make a big salad and homemade pizza," Melody replied.

"It'll be fun," Maddie said as she dropped her hand from Melody's. "Please, Daddy. We never do anything together and this will be fun."

"What time?" Hank asked.

"Why don't we say around six? What kind of pizza do you like, Maddi—Madeline?" Melody asked.

"Pepperoni is my favoritest."

"Then pepperoni it is," she replied.

"Okay, then we'll see you around six," Hank said. "And now, Maddie, it's time to go home."

"Bye, Melody," Maddie said.

"Goodbye, Madeline," Melody replied. She watched as father and daughter walked back out into the hallway. They didn't touch each other, didn't even speak, and Melody wondered about their relationship.

Which do you like better? Cowboys or bodyguards? If Melody had to hazard a guess, it would be that Maddie wasn't thrilled with her father's new job.

She returned to packing up the items in Lainie's room, thoughts of Maddie and Hank falling aside as her heart filled with memories of her sister. Each item that went into a box for charity broke her heart.

By ten o'clock she was exhausted. She took a quick shower, changed into her nightclothes then got into bed.

She tried not to be depressed that she'd learned

nothing over the last couple of days to help identify her sister's killer, but it was hard not to be discouraged.

Nobody seemed to know anything about the man Lainie was going out with on the night of her murder. Nobody knew anyone who was angry with her or wanted to harm her.

"I'm trying, Lainie. I'm trying to find out who took you from me," she whispered in the dark of the room. With her heart aching, she drifted off to sleep.

The ringing phone awakened her, and her first thought was that it was Lainie, calling to tell her about her day. She rolled over and fumbled on the nightstand for the receiver, at the same time waking up enough to know that it couldn't be Lainie.

Lainie was dead.

The luminous numbers on her clock radio let her know it was just after midnight. Who on earth would be calling at this time?

She grabbed the receiver and lifted it to her ear. "Hello?"

"Go back where you came from." The low, male, guttural voice was filled with a menace that seeped through the line.

Her first impulse was to hang up, and that's exactly what she did. She tossed the phone onto the bed and reached out to turn on the lamp, needing light as a chill danced up and down her spine.

Although the phone call had frightened her, it excited her at the same time because it meant she'd made somebody nervous. Now all she had to figure out was who.

* * *

Hank stood in the doorway of Maddie's room, watching her sleep. A knot formed in his chest as he stared at her little face.

She'd been angry with him ever since he'd made the decision to sell the ranch and move here. He didn't know how to deal with her anger and he didn't know how to deal with the fact that every time he looked at the daughter he loved, he remembered the woman he'd lost.

Something in him had died with Rebecca, something integral to life, and he didn't know how to reclaim it, wasn't even sure he wanted to try.

He moved away from the door and went into his room, where the king-size bed awaited him. It was late. He should be asleep, but sleep had been a problem for him ever since he'd sold the ranch.

Too little activity, he thought. He wished Dalton would call about a job, something that took him into dangerous territory where he had no time to think about himself or his life, where the only thing he had to worry about was survival.

He went back into the living room and poured himself a healthy shot of scotch, then sank down on the sofa to wait for sleep to claim him. More mornings than he cared to admit he woke up on the sofa, having never gone into the bedroom.

As he took a sip of the drink he realized that he felt as if he were waiting for his life to begin. From the moment he'd closed on the sale of the ranch he'd known that he was about to embark on a new life. But until Dalton came through with an assignment he was in limbo.

He frowned as he thought he heard a faint knock on his front door. A glance at the clock let him know it was after midnight. What the hell?

Setting his glass on the coffee table, he got up from the sofa and went to the door. He opened it a crack, surprised to see Melody standing on the other side. She was wrapped in a royal-blue bathrobe that matched her wide eyes and her hair was tousled as if she'd just climbed out of bed.

"Did I wake you?" she asked. "I thought I saw a light beneath your door. God, I hope I didn't wake you."

"I was still up." He opened the door wide enough to allow her to enter. "Is something wrong?" As she swept past him he caught a whiff of her scent, that slightly floral fragrance he found so attractive.

"I'm sorry to bother you. Nothing is really wrong, I just got a phone call and I couldn't go back to sleep and to be honest I just needed to talk to someone." She tied, then retied the belt around her waist.

He took her arm and led her to the sofa. "What kind of phone call?"

She sat on the edge of the sofa. "It was a man. He told me to go back where I came from."

Hank looked at her in surprise and sat next to her. "When did this happen?"

"Just a few minutes ago."

"Did you recognize the voice? Did you check the caller ID?"

"The call came up anonymous and no, I didn't recognize the voice." She wrapped her arms around herself, as if to ward off a bone-chilling shiver.

"I was just having a little scotch. Want one?" he asked.

She hesitated a moment, then nodded. "Okay, maybe just a little," she agreed.

He got up and poured her a finger of the amber liquid, then returned to sit next to her and handed her the small glass.

"Thanks. I didn't think the phone call bothered me that much, so after I hung up I shut off my light and tried to go back to sleep, but I kind of got creeped out." She took a sip of the scotch and grimaced. "This stuff always tastes like medicine to me."

He smiled. "It's good medicine. It will warm you up from the inside out."

She nodded and took another sip. "The good news is I guess I've got somebody nervous with all the questions I've been asking."

"Maybe now's the time to step back and let Zack West do his job," Hank replied.

Her eyes narrowed slightly and she set her glass on the coffee table next to his. "Not on your life. I'm getting closer and if it was Lainie's killer who contacted me, then maybe he'll call again and maybe he'll say something that will identify him to me."

"I don't like it," Hank said flatly. "Besides the people in the bar, who else have you spoken to about Lainie?"

"Yesterday I went to Hall's Car Haven and talked to Dean, but he wasn't any help." She frowned thoughtfully. "Maybe I just need to make a list of all the people I've talked to, and the killer will be on the list."

"You're forgetting one little thing," he replied. "Cotter Creek is a very small town. I'm sure everyone knows you've been asking questions."

"So it could be somebody I haven't even talked to," she replied with a frown.

"Have you changed the locks on the town house?" He stared down into his drink, finding the slender curve of her neck and the peek of something black and lacy just above the neckline of her robe disconcerting.

"Not yet. I meant to do it, but haven't gotten around to it. I'll do it first thing in the morning."

"Maybe you should stay here for the rest of the night." He looked at her once again and fought the impulse to reach out and stroke a length of her long, shiny hair.

"Thanks, but I don't think that's necessary. If he really wanted to harm me, then he wouldn't have called to warn me off."

Hank reluctantly agreed with her assessment. "Still, you've made yourself visible and that could be dangerous."

"Then maybe we should make your services to me official," she replied. "I don't know what the going rate for bodyguard services is, but I might be able to afford you for a little while."

"That isn't necessary," he replied. "I'm already on board." He wanted to demand that she stop asking questions, demand that she leave the investigation to the appropriate authorities. But he didn't have the right to demand anything of her and besides, he had a feeling it wouldn't do any good. She was determined, driven by some inner demon to find out the truth.

"Just do me a favor," he said. "Don't go asking questions of anyone else unless I'm with you."

She picked up her glass once again and studied him over the rim. "You're a nice man, Hank Tyler."

He wasn't a nice man. She'd had a scare, and all he could think about was taking her into his arms and discovering just how little she had on beneath her robe. He wanted to find out how that black lace molded to her breasts, then rip it off her to reveal her nakedness.

She tipped the glass to her lips and finished the last of the scotch. "I'm sorry for bothering you with this," she said as she stood. "The call freaked me out a little bit and I just needed somebody to talk to. I knocked softly, hoping if you were asleep I wouldn't bother you." Her cheeks grew pink, as if with a touch of embarrassment.

"Don't apologize, and anytime you feel frightened or upset, don't hesitate to knock as loud as you need to."

He stood as well and walked with her to the door, trying to think of a reason for her to stay longer. The nights had become so long lately.

When she reached the door she turned to look at him, her gratitude shining from her eyes. "Thanks, Hank."

"For what? For the scotch?"

She smiled. "No, for the company."

Without even realizing he intended to kiss her, he did. He leaned his head down, saw the widening of her eyes just before his lips touched hers.

Immediately she opened her mouth to him, as if she'd been expecting the kiss, as if she welcomed it. If she hadn't opened her mouth, the kiss would have been entirely different, but she did and Hank wound his arms around her, pulled her close and kissed her like he'd wanted to since the moment he'd first met her.

Her mouth was hot and tasted of the scotch and as his tongue swirled with hers, he was lost…lost in a whirlwind of desire that he hadn't felt for a very long time.

She molded against the length of him, her breasts snug against his chest. He wanted to rip the robe from her, carry her to his bed and make love to her until the sun came up.

Before he could follow through on any of the hundred things he'd have liked to do, she broke the kiss and stepped back from him with a gasp. Her lips trembled slightly and she gazed up at him with wide eyes.

"I'm sorry," he said and jammed his hands into his pockets. "That was totally unprofessional."

She ran a hand through her hair, as if giving herself time to steady, then offered him a little half smile that reignited a flame in the pit of his stomach. "Sometimes I like a man who isn't always professional."

Her words and the shine in her eyes did little to lessen the heat that burned him from the inside out, but he didn't want her to get the wrong idea. "Look, Melody, I'll confess that I'm very attracted to you."

"I'm attracted to you, too." Once again her cheeks filled with color.

"But I'm not interested in anything long-term. I had the one big love of my life and I'm not looking for another."

"As soon as Lainie's murderer is caught, I'm out of here. And even if he isn't caught by the end of summer, I have a life to go back to in Chicago," she replied. "I'm not looking for anything long-term, either, but if you're interested in a summer fling, then maybe we can talk about it."

She didn't wait for his reply. With her cheeks flaming bright red, she escaped out the door and went down the hall to Lainie's place.

Hank stared after her, torn between his desire for physical release and the need to hold someone warm and feminine in his arms—and a vague feeling that he was already in over his head as far as Melody Thompson was concerned.

Chapter 5

That kiss. That unexpected, sizzling kiss played in Melody's mind until sleep finally claimed her. And it was the first thing she thought of when she opened her eyes the next morning.

But the thought of the kiss didn't disturb her as much as her offer to him of a meaningless physical fling. Jeez, she thought as she showered, she'd practically offered herself up like a Thanksgiving turkey on a decorative platter.

Minutes later, dressed for the day, she sat at the kitchen table sipping coffee and preparing a list of things she needed to buy at the grocery store for the pizza party that night.

Even though she'd been awake more than half the night, it was just after seven and she felt remarkably rested. She was embarrassed by her forwardness the night before, but she was looking forward to spending the evening with Hank and Maddie.

By eight she'd finished her list, drunk her coffee and called a locksmith to change the locks she'd forgotten about until last night. He'd told her to expect him within the next hour. She then moved to Lainie's bedroom to continue the packing.

All the clothes and shoes were now in boxes neatly packed for donation. She'd stripped the bed, and all that was left were the personal items in the drawers and on top of the dresser.

She'd begun packing up the collection of fairies when she heard a knock on the door. It must be the locksmith, she thought as she hurried to answer.

She opened the door to a man wearing a paint-splattered apron and holding a can of paint. He was obviously not the locksmith. "Hi, I'm Mike. Fred sent me, said you needed a wall painted."

She'd told Fred that she could take care of it, but apparently Fred wanted to help. She would have preferred to do it herself, but she couldn't very well turn away the offer without appearing ungracious.

"Come on in," she said and pointed to the living room wall.

"Wow, kind of a shame to cover up a work of art," Mike said as he set the can of paint down next to him.

She smiled. "To you and me, maybe a work of art. To somebody who wants to buy this place it might be considered an eyesore."

"Guess you're right," he agreed. "I've got to go back

out to my truck and get some drop cloths and rollers. I'll be right back."

Reluctantly, Melody recognized it was probably for the best that Fred had sent Mike to help. She needed to get the place on the market as soon as possible and packing up Lainie's things was taking longer than she'd expected. Packing up memories always took longer than a person anticipated, she thought.

By the time Mike had all the furniture and floor covered with drop cloths, the locksmith had arrived and the morning passed with a flurry of activity.

When the locksmith left she felt a new sense of security. Nobody who Lainie had given a key to the town house would be getting in now. She wasn't giving a key to anyone.

Mike worked only an hour, then got a phone call and had to leave. He said he'd be back later that afternoon but she told him that would be inconvenient for her. She had shopping to do and pizza to make and she didn't want anyone in there while she prepared for the night with Hank and Maddie.

By two o'clock Melody had all the groceries she needed for the meal and began making the dough for the crust. She liked to cook, found it cathartic.

As she worked, her thoughts once again returned to Hank. She hoped he didn't think that she regularly offered herself up for meaningless affairs. She'd never done anything like that before. Maybe the stress she was under accounted for her intense attraction and her uncharacteristic forwardness to a man she hardly knew.

With the dough rising, she went into the living room

where she folded up the drop cloths Mike had put down and cleaned the room for company.

There had been little time for friendships in Melody's life. Lainie had taken the role of sister, friend and confidante, rarely leaving time for anyone else in Melody's life.

She'd begun to make friendships in Chicago, but there hadn't been time to foster anything deep and meaningful. For the first time in her life she wished she had a girlfriend, somebody she could call and talk to about Hank and the crazy feelings she was developing for him. But there was nobody. She had to navigate the uncharted waters of pure lust on her own.

By five o'clock she had everything ready for the oven and the salad made and chilling in the refrigerator. She took a long, leisurely shower, then put on a pink sundress and pulled her hair up into a ponytail.

A touch of mascara, a dab of lipstick and simple gold hoops in her ears and she was set for her evening of entertaining.

At precisely six, a knock sounded on the door and she answered to see Maddie and Hank. "We got cheesecake for dessert," Maddie said as she held a bakery box tight against her chest.

"Hmm, that's my favorite dessert after chocolate-chip cookies," Melody said as she took the box from Maddie. She smiled at Hank and instantly a ball of tension knotted up in her stomach.

That kiss.

The sight of him in his jeans and T-shirt, the scent of him as he walked past her into the living room, instantly evoked the memory of that kiss.

"Something smells good," Hank said. He smiled and in the heat of that smile she had a feeling he was remembering their late-night kiss as well.

"Pizza sauce," she said. "Come on into the kitchen. I've got everything ready but I thought Madeline might want to help me load the pizza before we pop it into the oven."

"Okay," she agreed with childish eagerness.

Within minutes they were all in the kitchen, Maddie and Melody at the counter and Hank seated at the table enjoying a cold beer.

"Daddy said you teach third grade," Maddie said as she decorated the pizza with slices of pepperoni.

"I do," Melody replied.

"So, you must like kids."

"Sure, I think kids are terrific," Melody said.

"Do you like to brush little girls' hair?" Maddie asked.

Melody shot a glance at Hank, who shrugged his shoulders to indicate he had no idea where the conversation was going. "Would you like me to brush your hair after we eat?" Melody asked.

"Maybe you could put it up in a ponytail like yours?" Maddie asked.

"I think I could manage that," Melody agreed.

For the next thirty minutes, as the pizza baked, they chatted about mundane things—favorite movies, favorite food and favorite things to do on lazy summer days.

For Melody it felt a bit like foreplay as she learned about the things Hank liked and didn't like. He loved watermelon but didn't like oranges. He enjoyed horseback riding and swimming but disliked jogging.

Maddie seemed to love everything and while they ate

their pizza and salad she kept them entertained with stories of friends from her school in Texas and all the places in town she and her grandmother had visited.

Melody found the interaction between Hank and his daughter strained. Hank seemed ill at ease around her and Maddie spent most of the evening talking to Melody.

After dinner they moved into the living room where Hank and Melody sat on the sofa and Maddie sat on the floor between Melody's legs so Melody could brush her silky, fine dark hair.

"My mommy used to brush my hair every night, but Grandma never has time and Daddy doesn't know how to do it right," Maddie said as Melody worked. Melody's heart squeezed with pain for the little girl who'd lost her mother.

"I see you've started working on painting," Hank said and gestured to the wildflowers on the wall that had been partially painted over.

"Fred sent over a painter to take care of it. He was just here for a little while this morning and is supposed to come back tomorrow to finish it."

"I can think of a few things I'd like to finish," he replied beneath his breath.

Just that easily the memory of their kiss exploded in her head and brought with it a tension that was palpable in the air between them.

"I want it just like yours," Maddie said, breaking the spell.

Melody pulled the last of Maddie's hair up and secured it with an elastic band. "There," she said. "Just like mine."

"Thanks." Maddie got up and ran to the hall mirror to admire her reflection.

"My mother is going to stop by here in a little while and get Maddie," he said. "She's going to spend the night with her grandma."

"Grandma promised me we'd watch my favorite movie tonight," Maddie said as she ran back into the living room.

"That sounds like fun," Melody replied, still intensely aware of Hank seated next to her.

Maddie reached up and touched her ponytail. "Do I look like a cowgirl?"

"Like Annie Oakley herself," Melody replied.

"Who is Annie Oakley?" Maddie asked.

The conversation that followed was about famous cowgirls and cowboys and by the time they'd finished with that, Hank's mother arrived at the door.

Susan Tyler was an attractive woman with Hank's blue eyes, a mop of graying dark hair and a friendly smile. She introduced herself to Melody with a firm handshake. "Maddie and Hank have been telling me all about you," she said. "I'm so sorry about your sister."

"Thank you. I've been enjoying the company of your granddaughter over the last couple of days."

Susan smiled and cast a look of obvious love at Maddie. "I've told her she's like a building rat, scurrying around here and there. I think she knows more gossip about the people in this building than anyone."

"Mrs. Walker wears a wig," Maddie quipped. "And Mr. Walker drinks too much."

Susan laughed. "See what I mean?" She motioned to the little girl. "Come on, honey. Let's go watch that movie of yours. It was nice to finally meet you, Melody." With that she and Maddie went out the door, leaving Melody alone with Hank.

He smiled at her, a lazy heated smile that warmed her from the top of her head to the tips of her toes. "Now, how about we finish what we started last night."

Hank had been on a slow simmer since she'd left his door the night before. The simmer had continued throughout this evening. As he'd watched her brushing Maddie's hair he'd wanted to reach out and release Melody's long dark hair from its band, feel the silky strands fall through his fingers and spill over his palms.

The sundress she wore emphasized her slender curves and exposed just enough skin to keep his imagination working overtime. As they'd eaten pizza, as they'd talked about everyday things, all he could think about was her offer for a meaningless summer fling.

"Did you mean what you said last night or was it just nerves talking?" he asked as she rejoined him on the sofa.

"You mean about being attracted to you? About being open for an uncommitted relationship?" She didn't meet his gaze, but rather stared down at her hands in her lap, nerves jangling in her stomach.

He reached for one of her hands, and it was only then that her gaze met his. "It wasn't nerves," she said. "And I meant what I said, but I want you to know that I don't go around offering myself to men like this on a regular basis." Her cheeks filled with color.

He loved the fact that she blushed. He found that tell-tale color in her cheeks charming. "I know that," he replied. He released her hand and leaned back, not want-ing to rush her, rush anything between them. "It's been a long time since I've had any kind of a relationship with any woman."

"How long has your wife been gone?"

"Two years. She died of breast cancer." His voice felt strained even to his own ears.

She was quiet for a moment. "That's a long time to be alone," she finally replied.

"I'm not alone. I have Maddie."

She frowned. "Not that it's any of my business, but she seems to be angry with you."

"She is." His heart constricted as it always did when he thought of his daughter. "She doesn't want me to take the job with Wild West Protective Services. She's been angry with me since I sold our ranch and she certainly isn't shy about telling anyone who will listen."

She smiled. "She doesn't seem to be shy about much of anything. Now I understand a question she asked me the other day."

"What question was that?"

"Which I liked better, cowboys or bodyguards," she replied.

Hank winced. "She's made it clear to me that she prefers cowboys. I just hope she stops being angry with me before she reaches the volatile teen years."

Melody laughed, then sobered slightly. "It's obvious she loves you very much."

"She's my heart," he replied gruffly, surprised by the wealth of emotion that suddenly rose up in the back of his throat.

Needing to get his daughter out of his head, he leaned over and touched the band securing her ponytail. "Do you mind? I've been thinking about letting your hair down all evening."

"I don't mind," she said, her voice a little bit breathless.

Gently he pulled the cloth-covered elastic band from her hair, relishing the feel as the silky strands tumbled down around her shoulders and into his hands. "You have beautiful hair," he said.

"I always wanted to be a blonde," she said as he continued to caress her hair and her shoulders. The bare skin of her shoulders was warm and achingly soft beneath his fingers. "You know, blondes have more fun and all that." She leaned her head forward as his hands smoothed across the back of her neck. "Although at the moment I can't imagine a blonde in the world who is having more fun than me."

He leaned in and placed his lips against the warm skin of her neck. "And I can't think of a blonde in the world I want to be with right now," he murmured.

He knew they were moving too fast, but he didn't care and she didn't seem to care either. He didn't want consequences in the morning or in the days to come from whatever happened here tonight, but his want of her was greater than his good sense.

She turned in his arms to face him and he saw that the fire in her eyes matched the heat that burned in his groin. "We really don't know each other well enough to even be considering this," she said.

"You're right," he agreed as he dragged his index finger over her lips.

Her eyes flared darker. "I'm not looking for a relationship," she said when his finger moved to the soft skin of her cheek. "I have a life to get back to."

"I told you last night, I'm not looking for anything lasting," he said. "I'd say for right now, for this moment, we're perfect for each other."

It was she who leaned forward for the kiss, a kiss that answered any doubts he might have entertained. As he pulled her closer to him she wrapped her arms around his neck. His tongue danced with hers and his desire grew more intense.

He located the source of that dizzying scent just behind her ear and along the slender column of her throat. He ran his mouth across her skin, nipping with his teeth as she gasped with delight.

She finally pulled away from him. He immediately dropped his hands to his sides, unsure if she wanted to continue and unwilling to pressure her in any way.

"I have to know that this won't change anything between us," she said. "You're my only friend here in town, and I need a friend."

"You've got one," Hank replied and he meant it. Hell, at the moment he'd agree to almost anything to get her into the bedroom.

She stood suddenly and held out her hand to him. Hank's heart jumped into his throat as he also rose and took her hand in his.

Without saying a word she led him down the hall to a bedroom with a double bed. The only light in the room was from a dim lamp on the nightstand and the play of light and shadow created an intimate aura.

Someplace in the back of his mind he knew what was happening, that somehow fate had brought together two people in need. Melody was reeling from the death of her sister and he had been alone long enough to feel an aching loneliness that begged for the comfort of a warm, willing body next to his.

He reached for her and she came back into his arms. He thought he felt a hint of desperation as she molded herself against him, as if she were seeking to warm a place in herself that had been cold for a very long time.

He kissed her again, this time softly, tenderly, wishing to find that place inside her and heat it. At the same time his fingers moved to the zipper of her sundress. He moved the zipper down only an inch or so, then paused and waited to see if she'd call a halt to things.

When she didn't, he unzipped the dress all the way down. His hands found the warm skin of her back and he splayed his fingers against it, loving the way it felt.

She moved her hands up beneath his T-shirt, her fingers cool as they explored the width of his back. Still their kiss continued, growing less tender and more urgent.

Her dress slipped from her shoulders and she allowed it to fall to the floor. At the same time Hank stepped back from her and pulled his T-shirt over his head.

For a long moment they stared at each other. She looked hot in her white bikini pants and lacy bra. Her nipples were taut against the lace and her lips were swollen from his kisses.

"Are you sure you want to go on?" he asked, his voice thick with desire. As difficult as it would be, if she wanted to call a halt to things, he'd get dressed again and leave without thinking any less of her.

In answer to his question she got into the bed and opened her arms to him. A sizzling electricity shot through him as pulled a condom from his pocket then shucked off his jeans and joined her beneath the sheets, the foil package on the nightstand.

Once again they were in each other's arms, kissing with a hunger that chased every other thought out of his head. He told himself that in his present state of mind it wouldn't have mattered who he held in his arms, that all he needed was the release of having sex with any woman.

But deep inside he knew that wasn't true. It wasn't just her feminine scent and her physical attractiveness that made him want her. Rather it was a combination of that and her unwavering loyalty to the memory of her sister, the gentle way she'd brushed Maddie's hair and her laughter as they'd strung cheese down their chins while eating pizza.

Her body was hot against his and he relished the heat and the smoothness of her skin as they clung together. Within minutes the last of their clothes were gone and they began to explore each other with hands and mouths.

Hank wanted to take her fast and furious, not giving himself time to think, time to breathe, but with a surprising sense of command she set the pace…slow and leisurely and excruciatingly intense.

Her mouth moved down his jaw and neck, down to his chest and he gasped as every muscle in his body tensed. The silky strands of her hair teased him at the same time her warm lips tortured him.

He was only willing to be a passive participant for so long. He wanted to taste her skin, to hear soft breathless moans escape from her lips.

He rolled her over on her back, taking command of the situation. His hands cupped her breasts, thumbs grazing over the tips, and she mewled with pleasure.

He captured one of her nipples in his mouth, sucking and rolling his tongue around it. She tangled her hands in his hair, pulled him closer, closer still, as if afraid he might stop.

His blood surged thick and hot as his hand moved down her stomach and touched her intimately. Gasping, she tightened her hands in his hair. When his fingers began to move against her, rubbing in a rhythmic pattern, she arched her hips up to meet his touch.

His excitement rose as she writhed and moaned with pleasure. Every muscle in her body tensed as her moans grew louder, higher pitched and then she cried out and shuddered.

Gasping breaths followed as she reached to encircle his hardness with her hand. He closed his eyes, not wanting to look into hers, not wanting to emotionally connect in any way. He wanted to keep this all about the sex, all about the simple act of physical release. He didn't want to want Melody. He just wanted to want the warmth of her body, the uncomplicated sex act without baggage.

He gasped again as she stroked the length of him and he throbbed, barely maintaining control. As if she knew how precariously close he was to losing it, she removed her hand from him and instead reached across him to pick up the foil packet from the nightstand.

He took it from her, knowing that if she touched him again he'd explode. It took only seconds to pull on the condom then he crouched above her, between her thighs and entered her.

Her midnight-blue eyes drew him in as their gazes locked. In that moment the deep, painful loneliness that had plagued him for the past two years ebbed and for just a moment an edge of happiness fluttered inside his chest.

With that flutter came a crashing sense of guilt and he slammed his eyes closed and gave himself to the physical sensations her wet warmth evoked in him.

Her fingers clutched at his back as he plunged into her and all civility fell away as he took her with hunger and demand.

Meeting him thrust for thrust, she was wild and abandoned beneath him, raking her fingers first across his back and then grabbing his buttocks to pull him in deeper, harder.

The tension inside him built to impossible heights and the last of his control slipped away at the same time she cried out and tensed beneath him. Knowing she'd climaxed, he allowed himself to let go, a hoarse groan escaping him as his release crashed through him.

He collapsed to the side of her, his heart pounding more ferociously than he could ever remember. His breaths began to slow at the same time as Melody's and within minutes their breathing had returned to normal.

She rolled over to her side and looked at him. He knew he should say something, but an awkward silence grew between them. She finally broke it. "Are you okay?" she asked softly.

He smiled. "I'd say I'm more than okay. What about you?"

She returned his smile. "I'm more than okay." Her smile fell slightly as she continued to hold his gaze. "This was probably a mistake, wasn't it?"

"Why do you say that?"

She sat up and clutched the sheet to her chest, a frown dancing between her eyebrows. "I need you as a friend and as a support in trying to find Lainie's killer. I don't want things to get weird between us, Hank."

"Things won't get weird," he assured her, but even as he spoke the words he felt the need to get up, to escape from those dark, drowning eyes of hers, eyes so unlike the woman whose memory was burned into his heart.

Melody leaned forward and kissed him on the cheek, her lips soft and pleasurable against his skin. "I'll be right back."

She slid out of bed and he watched her as she walked across the room, her naked skin looking smooth and touchable in the soft lighting. She disappeared out of the bedroom and he heard the closing of the bathroom door in the master bedroom.

Instantly he was up and out of the bed. He grabbed his clothes and dashed into the bathroom across the hall—the bathroom where Lainie had been killed. It took him only minutes to clean up and get dressed, then he went out to the living room and waited for Melody to find him.

A few moments later she came into the living room clad in the same robe she'd been wearing when she'd come to his apartment after receiving the disturbing phone call. The material clung to her naked curves, and with her hair tousled and her lips still slightly swollen she looked so hot he felt a stirring of new desire.

He didn't want to just run out the door, but again the need to escape from her presence was nearly overwhelming. "Thanks for the pizza party," he said. "And for being so nice to my daughter."

Melody smiled. "It's easy to be nice to Maddie. She's a beautiful, charming little girl. If I made a short pot of coffee, would you drink a cup with me?"

He opened his mouth to decline but before the words came out, the window just behind Melody exploded.

Chapter 6

A short, sharp scream burst from Melody as she flung herself forward, away from the shattering glass. Hank caught her in his arms and pulled her behind him as if to shield her from any danger that might come barreling through the window.

The crash of glass was followed by utter silence. On the floor just inside the window was a midsize red brick. Seconds ticked by and neither of them moved, then Hank stepped forward and grabbed the brick.

"Somebody definitely wants to get your attention," he said and held up the brick so she could see the words painted in bold black letters on one side.

GO HOME.

A streak of ice walked up her back, creating a shiver as she wrapped her arms around herself. Any glowing warmth that had been created by making love with Hank vanquished beneath the chill that possessed her now.

"Get dressed," Hank said flatly, his midnight-blue eyes narrowed to dangerous slits. "I'm going to call the sheriff."

Melody nodded and went back to the bedroom. Her clothes were scattered around the room. In a daze, she got dressed, and by the time she was fully clad the initial shock had worn off.

She was obviously making somebody very nervous with her questions and probing. But who? She was no closer now to finding out the identity of Lainie's murderer than she'd been the minute she'd arrived in town. What was she missing? Who had she made so nervous?

By the time she returned to the living room Hank was pacing in front of the sofa, his handsome features set in cold sternness. "Zack should be here in a few minutes," he said. "It's too late to get a glass place out here tonight so I called Dalton. He's going to bring over some plywood so we can secure the window for the rest of the night."

"Thanks," she said.

He smiled, the gesture not quite reaching his eyes. "You sure know how to show a guy a good time. Pizza, sex and danger, one hell of a night."

She smiled. "I wouldn't mind repeating the first two, but I could do without the danger part."

This time he didn't return her smile. "Anonymous phone calls are one thing. Those are usually made by cowards who shy away from any real confrontation. But this is a definite escalation."

At that moment Zack West arrived. It took him only minutes to assess the situation. He frowned as Hank showed him the brick, then Zack turned his attention to her. "What cages have you been rattling since you've been in town?"

"All I've been doing is asking questions of some of Lainie's friends and acquaintances," she replied.

"She got a threatening phone call last night," Hank said. "Somebody told her to get out of town."

"And the caller ID?" Zack asked.

"Anonymous, of course," Melody said.

"Of course," he replied. He swiped a hand through his dark hair and frowned again. "I'm sure whoever threw that brick through the window is long gone. I'll check around outside but I doubt I'll find anything. I'll write up a report of both this incident and the phone call. If anything else happens contact me immediately. Unfortunately, there isn't much else I can do."

Melody certainly hadn't expected anything else. As Hank walked Zack to the door, she went into the kitchen and got a broom to clean up as much of the broken glass as possible.

It's just a broken window, she thought. It wasn't like she'd been personally attacked. Hank had said it was an escalation, but as far as she was concerned bricks through the window were in the same category as anonymous callers.

"Where's your vacuum?" Hank asked when Zack had left.

"In the hall closet," she replied.

For the next few minutes they worked together, she

sweeping and he vacuuming. It was impossible to talk above the roar of the vacuum.

It was after two in the morning when Dalton finished putting the plywood in the window and he and Hank left. Melody returned to her bedroom and changed into her nightgown, then crawled into the bed that still smelled of Hank.

As she lay there in the darkness of the night she thought of making love with Hank. It had been amazing. He'd been a demanding but thoughtful lover, taking her over the edge not once, but twice, before allowing himself his release.

She'd felt safe in his arms, connected enough that the terrible void Lainie's death had left had been momentarily filled.

But now, alone in the deep of night, the pain of loss was nearly overwhelming. She imagined that it was what a mother felt when she lost a child, for in many ways Lainie had been her child.

The thought of never seeing Lainie again, of never answering the phone and hearing the sound of her voice, constricted Melody's heart so painfully she was crying before she knew it.

The sobs ripped from someplace deep inside her and it was as if each tear that fell tore away a piece of her aching heart.

She buried her face in her pillow and didn't attempt to stop the sobs, but rather let them consume her. She cried for all the things she'd never again share with her sister. She wept for all the experiences and dreams shared but not fulfilled.

When night falls, monsters creep out of the shadows and one of those monsters had crept out of the darkness and stolen Lainie...from Melody.

"I'll get you," she whispered. "Somehow, someway I'll find out who you are and make you pay." No broken window or threatening phone calls were going to scare her away. She was going to find out who killed Lainie. With this driving need burning in her heart, she finally fell asleep.

She awoke early, with thoughts of Hank flitting around in her head. His clean, slightly spicy cologne still hung faintly on the sheets.

If she hadn't felt such a horrifying emptiness, would she have tumbled into bed with him so easily? Somehow she doubted it. But she'd been so incredibly physically attracted to him...and lonely. And if she looked deep inside herself, she knew she'd see more than just a little bit of fear.

She didn't know how to live without Lainie. Her sister had filled her hours even after Melody had moved to Chicago. Worrying about Lainie, thinking about Lainie, had become such a habit and she had nothing to take the place of that habit.

For a few minutes the night before, when she'd been in Hank's arms, she'd forgotten her heartache. The loneliness had disappeared and she'd been filled with him.

But this morning, with the bright sunshine streaking through the window, came the knowledge that falling into bed with Hank had been a dumb thing to do.

As she pulled herself out of bed and went into the bathroom in the master bedroom, she hoped that things wouldn't be awkward when she saw him again.

It was after nine by the time she'd showered and sat at the table with her first cup of coffee. Mike was supposed to return sometime this morning to finish painting the wall in the living room. Melody had arranged for a local charity to come that afternoon to get some of the boxes of clothing she'd packed and the furniture from Lainie's bedroom.

She had yet to go into the bathroom where Lainie had been killed, although she knew that sooner or later she was going to have to pack up whatever items were in there. But the idea of going in there, of standing in the last place that Lainie had stood alive, horrified her.

"Not today," she told herself as she got up to pour herself another cup of coffee. She still had to call somebody about replacing the glass in the living room, then later tonight she wanted to make a trip to the video store. She'd called the store earlier in the week to find out James O'Donnell's schedule. It was Friday and she knew James would be working. He was the only loose end on her short list of suspects.

A knock on the door pulled her out of her chair. She answered to find Hank's mother, Susan. "I hope I'm not intruding," she said.

"Not at all. I was just having some coffee." Melody opened the door wider to allow her to step inside. "Would you like to join me?"

"That would be nice," Susan agreed.

As Melody led the way to the kitchen she wondered what Hank's mother was doing here. She was amused to realize that she felt like a guilty teenager caught by a disapproving mother.

Susan sat at the table and Melody poured her a cup of coffee, then joined her there. "I just wanted you to be aware of how much Maddie loved your sister," she began.

Melody's heart squeezed tight and she realized the tears of the night before hadn't emptied the well of her sorrow. "Lainie was special," she replied.

Susan nodded, her graying hair sparkling in the sunshine coming in through the nearby window. "When Hank and Maddie moved here, Maddie wasn't just a little girl mourning the loss of her mother. She was also mourning the loss of a lifestyle and, more important, the absence of her father."

Susan paused to sip the coffee and then set the cup down and continued. "Physically, Hank was there, but emotionally he withdrew from everything when Rebecca died, including his daughter."

She leaned back in the chair and a wistful smile played on her lips. "There was magic with Hank and Rebecca. They'd been high school sweethearts and there was no question that they were meant to be together." The smile fell away. "When Rebecca died something died inside Hank. For a while, I didn't think he'd ever laugh again for the rest of his life. But when he moved in here and met Lainie I saw sparks of life returning to him. She made him laugh."

Melody smiled. "For all the problems Lainie had, a sense of humor was one of her strong suits."

Susan took a sip of her coffee once again and eyed Melody over the rim of the cup. "I see more than a spark of life in his eyes when he's around you."

"We're just friends," Melody said quickly. "He's

helping me get through some things, but it's nothing more than that." She didn't want Hank's mother to think that Hank and Maddie had any real place in her life, nor she in theirs. "I'm returning to Chicago as soon as I get things straightened out here."

Susan's smile faltered slightly. "That's too bad. Maddie has grown quite fond of you."

"I'm still calling her Madeline because she doesn't know yet if we're going to be friends or not," Melody said with a small laugh.

"That little scamp," Susan replied, her love for her granddaughter obvious in her tone. "Hank tells me you're a teacher."

Melody nodded. "And I love it."

"You want children of your own?"

Melody leaned back in her seat, feeling as if she were being interviewed for a potential job. "Someday. I'm in no hurry. When I meet the right man and we decide together that it's time to start a family."

Susan drained her coffee cup and stood. "Well, I've taken up enough of your time. I just wanted to let you know how much I appreciate you giving Maddie some of your time. I worry about her, you know. I love the role of grandma, but she seems to need more than I can give her in that role. I'm afraid Hank will never let go of his grief and have another real relationship with a woman who can give Maddie what she needs."

"I'm sure they'll be fine," Melody said, although she had no idea if that was the case or not. "Hank seems like a great guy. Eventually he'll find that woman he can have magic with again."

"I hope so," Susan said fervently. "I just want to see my son and my granddaughter happy again."

When Susan had left, Melody washed the cups and put them into the dishwasher and thought about magic. There hadn't been time in her life for magic with a man. She'd hoped that she'd eventually meet somebody in Chicago who would be special to her, but there hadn't been time.

She'd been so busy unpacking, settling in and starting the new job, so busy maintaining contact with Lainie and making sure that she was doing okay without Melody that dating had seemed like a far-fetched idea and finding somebody special virtually impossible.

Maybe that's why she had connected so quickly with Hank, because she'd sensed the grief that was still very much a part of his soul, and the grief inside her had recognized his.

One thing was clear. From what Susan had said, Hank definitely wasn't the man to provide magic. To him, she was nothing more than a momentary respite from his pain and he was nothing more than that to her.

The rest of the morning flew by. Mike arrived and began painting and the two men from Cotter Creek Charity Services came to take away the items from Lainie's bedroom.

With each piece of furniture that went out the door, Melody felt her heart tearing into little pieces. It was the final goodbye to her sister.

After the men left, her phone rang. She grabbed it to hear Hank's voice. "Maddie has insisted that we go out to eat at the café this evening and I thought you could be our guest. You know, kind of a payback for the pizza party last night."

"That isn't necessary," she replied, having every intention of declining the offer.

"Please come," he said. "Maddie will be so disappointed if you don't. Besides, you have to eat dinner somewhere, it might as well be while enjoying our company."

"All right," she heard herself saying despite her intentions to the contrary.

"Great, we'll pick you up around six. Will that work?"

"Perfect, but I have a request. Could we stop by the video store on the way to the café? There's a movie I'd like to rent."

Her words were followed by a long moment of silence. "I'd thought that after last night you might have changed your mind about doing any more investigating."

"A little brick through a window isn't going to stop me," she said with unexpected forcefulness. She drew a deep breath then continued. "Besides, James O'Donnell is the only person I have left on my list to talk to."

"Are you expecting a confession?"

"Of course not." But his question made her wonder just what she hoped to gain. "But maybe I'll see something in his eyes that will be guilt, or maybe he'll know something about somebody who might have been responsible."

"I'll take you into the video store to talk to this guy on one condition," Hank said. "When you're finished talking to him, you put it all behind you for the duration of our dinner."

"Deal," she agreed.

The afternoon flew by. The man from the glass shop

arrived to replace the broken window, Mike finished up the painting and before she knew it, it was time to get ready for the evening ahead.

After the chat with Susan, she'd thought it best to put some distance between herself and Hank and Maddie, but her brain had not engaged before her mouth had accepted the invitation to dinner.

A simple meal out, she told herself as she pulled on a red-and-white-flowered sundress. Red sandals and earrings completed the outfit. Casual and comfortable, she thought as she applied her makeup with a deft hand.

At precisely six her doorbell rang and she hurried to answer. "Daddy says I can order two desserts tonight," Maddie said. Dressed in a pair of navy shorts and a red-and-navy top, Maddie looked like the all-American girl.

"Only if you eat a vegetable with your meal," Hank said as he smiled in greeting to Melody. "Hi. Are you ready?" He was dressed casual. His worn jeans snuggled against the length of his legs and a navy T-shirt clung to his broad shoulders.

She was surprised by a tiny flutter in her stomach at the sight of him. "Just let me grab my purse," she said. She picked up her purse from the sofa, then together the three of them left the town house.

"Daddy says we're stopping at the video store and I can pick out a movie to take home and watch," Maddie said as she walked close to Melody's side.

"Have you decided already what movie you want to see?"

"Maybe something about a horse. I love horses," Maddie replied.

"I'll try to help you find something really good," Melody offered and was rewarded with a bright smile from the little girl.

"How was your day?" Hank asked once they were all settled in his car and driving toward the café.

"Busy," she replied. "I had the window replaced, and Mike finished painting the wall. Unfortunately, with that wall newly painted, I think he's going to have to come back and do the other walls in the living room. The other three look kind of shabby now. Men from Cotter Creek Charity came and took most of the things from the master bedroom. Slowly but surely I'm getting things done. What about you? Busy day?"

She suddenly found herself wondering what he did during the days and nights. He didn't have an official job. So, how did he spend his time?

"About like all the other days. Mom had Maddie so I went down to the shooting range and practiced. I checked in with Dalton and hung out at the Wild West Protective Services office, then took care of a little financial business on the computer." He shrugged. "At the moment my days aren't the stuff that movies are made about."

"Actually, your mother stopped in this morning to visit me."

He glanced at her and crooked one of his dark brows upward. "And was that a good thing?"

Melody laughed. "Of course. Should I have worried about it being a bad thing?"

"Not really, but since we've moved here she's become more of a hands-on mother than I'd have ever guessed her to be."

"She just wants you to be happy," Melody said softly.

"Yeah, well, wouldn't it be nice if we could all be happy," he said, and she thought she heard a touch of bitterness in his voice.

The rest of the ride to the video store was filled with Maddie talking about her favorite movies and what desserts she intended to order after their meal.

"I'm thinking of ice cream and cookies, or maybe a piece of pie and a piece of cake," Maddie said.

"How about you think of what kind of vegetable you want to eat first," Hank said with a conspiratorial grin at Melody.

"Personally my favorite is brussels sprouts," Melody said.

"Yuck!" Hank and Maddie said in unison.

Melody laughed. "Just kidding. But, I do like broccoli or corn."

"Corn. That's good. I like corn," Maddie said, decision made.

By the time they reached the video store a small knot of tension had formed in Melody's chest. According to Hank, Lainie had complained of James O'Donnell stalking her. If that were true, he not only might know details of Lainie's life that nobody else knew, but he was also the most viable suspect Melody had.

A rivulet of fear slithered up her back as she thought of James O'Donnell.

Hank parked the car in front of the store and shut off

the engine, but before leaving the car he turned to look at her. "You ready for this?"

She offered him a shaky smile. "As ready as I'm going to get."

"Just don't forget I'm here for you." He reached across the seat and grabbed her hand in his, and for a moment his gaze connected with hers in a way that felt like magic.

And that scared her almost as much as the idea of standing face-to-face with the man who might have killed Lainie.

Chapter 7

Hank had awakened that morning with the scent of Melody clinging to his skin, the heat of her lips burned into his. He'd spent most of his day trying not to think about what they'd shared the night before, shutting her out of his mind while he tried to fill his head with thoughts of the woman he'd lost.

When Maddie had asked for Melody to join them for dinner, he'd wanted to tell her no, but one look from his daughter's pleading eyes and he knew he couldn't deny her request. He'd intended to keep his distance from Melody, to enjoy a pleasant dinner without feeling anything for her.

But the moment she'd opened her door, his heart had jumped. Now, as they got out of the car to go inside the video store, he was surprised to discover a protective surge building up inside him where she was concerned.

He knew O'Donnell on sight, had seen him lurking around the town houses from time to time, and Lainie had pointed him out as a creep she'd been nice to but couldn't get rid of.

When they walked inside the store, he saw only a female clerk behind the counter. James O'Donnell was nowhere in sight. Maddie hurried over to the children's section near the register. While she looked for a video, Hank could keep an eye on her while standing at the register.

"Is James O'Donnell here?" Melody asked the woman by the cash register, who wore a badge that indicated her name was Linda.

"He's in the back stocking," Linda said with a snap of the gum she was chewing loudly.

"Could we speak to him?" Melody asked.

Linda shrugged. "Hey, James!" she yelled. "Need you up front."

A minute later James O'Donnell appeared in the doorway that led to a back room. O'Donnell was tall, a bit overweight and had a patch of acne scars on one cheek. His oily brown hair was in need of a haircut and his eyes widened slightly at the sight of Melody.

Hank stepped closer to her, close enough to smell the spicy scent of her perfume, feel the heat radiating from her body.

"Can I help you?" James asked, his gaze not wavering from Melody.

Hank felt the tension that rolled off Melody as James continued to stare at her, and he wanted to wrap his arm around her, claim her as his own so that

James would stop looking at her with those dark, hungry eyes.

"I'd like to talk to you about Lainie Thompson," Melody said.

"You're her sister, aren't you?" James said. "You look a lot like her."

"Yes, I'm her sister, Melody. I was wondering if maybe you knew something that would help us find out who murdered her?"

Dark shutters seemed to fall over his eyes, giving him an almost reptilian look. "I told the cops I don't know anything about anything. She put a restraining order against me a month before she died. I wasn't supposed to be anywhere near her."

"But I saw you around the town houses the week that she died," Hank interjected.

A dull red crept up James's neck. "I just wanted to see her. I didn't bother her any. I didn't bother anyone."

"Do you have any idea who she had a date with on the night she died?" Melody asked. Hank glanced over to Maddie, who was still looking at the juvenile movies, then he returned his gaze to James. The man gave him the creeps. There was something not quite right in the depths of his eyes.

He reached a hand up and picked at a pimple on his face. "She was supposed to go out with Forest Burke, but he stood her up." His eyes narrowed to small slits. "I didn't mention it to the sheriff, but I was kind of hanging around that night. I left about ten and she was still home."

"You didn't see anyone going into her place?"

Melody's voice held a faint plea, and the tension Hank had felt earlier wafting off her grew more intense.

Hank placed a hand on the small of her back to ground her, to keep her anchored as he felt her emotions intensify.

"You don't know anything about her murder? Maybe you went to see her after work and you fought with her? Did you hurt her, James?" She leaned over the counter. "Was it a terrible accident?"

James didn't back away or even flinch. "I would have never hurt Lainie. I loved her. Eventually we would have been together. She would have realized that we were meant for each other."

"Daddy, I want this one." Maddie broke the moment by dancing up beside Hank, a video in her hand.

Hank took the video and set it on the counter, then touched Melody's arm. "I think we're done here."

The female clerk checked them out as James walked to the back room. He didn't go inside, but rather stood by the door and stared at Melody in a way that made Hank want to punch the creep in the face.

As they left the store, Hank pulled Melody against him on one side and Maddie on the other, his arms around both of their shoulders.

"I feel like I need a shower," Melody muttered as they got into the car.

"Why?" Maddie asked from the backseat. "You don't look dirty or sweaty."

"I just feel a little bit icky," Melody replied.

"Sometimes when I feel icky chocolate ice cream makes me feel not icky," Maddie replied.

Melody laughed, the sound easing the knot of tension

in Hank's chest. "At the moment a big bowl of choco-late ice cream sounds terrific."

He knew she was disappointed by the talk with James, but as they got settled at a table in the café she seemed to put it behind her.

Her eyes sparkled as she chatted with Maddie, discussing the finer points of a video game Hank had never heard of. Hank found himself watching her covetously. He'd thought that in having sex with her he wouldn't want her anymore. But nothing could be further from the truth.

As she sat across from him and Maddie, he felt a resurgence of desire begin in the pit of his stomach. Each time she flipped a strand of that luxurious dark hair over her shoulder, he remembered how it had felt draped across his skin. Every time she licked her lips, the memory of what that tongue had done to him shot hot blood through his veins.

Was it any wonder? he thought. Until last night it had been a hell of a long time since he'd been with any woman. Was it any wonder that being with her had reminded him of how good a warm body could feel against his, how much he liked sex and had missed it?

She'd certainly made it clear to him that she wasn't looking for a relationship. She'd be out of his life in a matter of weeks, and that made her safe as far as he was concerned. That element of safety—no strings attached—made him want her as much as anything.

"You're very quiet," Melody said as she cut into her chicken-fried steak.

"Just relaxing," he replied. And imagining tasting every inch of your body, he thought to himself.

"Tell me about the ranch you used to own," she said.

"Daddy was the best cowboy in the whole world," Maddie exclaimed. Her lower lip thrust out into a pout. "And he should still be a cowboy, not a bodyguard."

Maddie didn't know about grief. She couldn't understand that the ranch had been something he and Rebecca had built together, and once his wife was gone none of it had meant anything anymore.

His grief had been too deep, his life ripped to shreds, and even now, thinking of the ranch and what he'd once had, filled a pool of sorrow inside him.

"There really isn't much to say about it," he answered. "I owned a ranch and now I don't." He heard the finality in his words that indicated there was nothing more to talk about on this particular subject.

He was grateful that Melody took his hint and instead, with Maddie's prompting, began to talk a little bit about her childhood.

"Lainie and I were like two musketeers, always together and always watching out for one another. We weren't just sisters, we were very best friends." A soft smile lit up her face, and Hank wanted to be welcomed into her memories.

"I wish I had a sister," Maddie exclaimed. "I don't even have a best friend."

Melody smiled and leaned forward to take one of Maddie's little hands in hers. "Wait until school starts. You're going to have so many wonderful new friends you won't know what to do."

The smile that Maddie gave Melody constricted Hank's heart. When was the last time his daughter had gazed at him so lovingly? And when was the last time he'd talked to her in any meaningful way?

The familiar grief of Rebecca's loss teased around the edges of his consciousness. There was a part of him that wanted to embrace it, wanted to wrap it around him to keep him insulated from any other hurt.

But at that moment, Melody and Maddie's laughter formed a joyous circle that beckoned him with the promise of happiness. Just for tonight, with his daughter and this beautiful woman across from him, he wanted to forget what had come before and simply enjoy the moment.

It had taken a while after leaving the video store for the chill of James O'Donnell to wear off Melody. But as the meal progressed it was impossible to maintain that icy cold pond inside her with Hank's gaze warming her from head to toe and Maddie's charming chatter filling her head.

It would have been easy to imagine the three of them as a family, out for an evening meal, then going home where she would tuck Maddie in with a good-night kiss and make love to Hank until the sun came up.

But she knew those were foolish thoughts. He'd made it clear he wasn't interested in anything permanent. He'd had his magic and apparently once in a lifetime was enough for him.

Still, as the evening progressed and Hank loosened up in a way she hadn't seen before, she was charmed and reluctant for the evening to end.

"You have to have dessert," Maddie said when the waitress had taken away their dinner plates.

"Yes, you have to have dessert," Hank agreed with a

lazy grin. "Maddie says, and we all know Maddie is the boss." Maddie giggled.

"Then by all means, I'll have dessert," Melody replied with a laugh. She ordered a piece of chocolate pie. Hank ordered apple cobbler and Maddie got both a banana split and a piece of cake.

As they ate, the conversation turned to Cotter Creek and the changes that had occurred over the nine months that Melody had been gone.

"I thought Wild West Protective Services was strictly a family business," she said. "I'm surprised they're hiring new people."

"From what Dalton told me, his brothers and sister have all chosen new paths. They're all married now and starting families and don't want to travel like they used to," Hank replied. "Dalton told me he wants to hire at least five more men who will be based here in Cotter Creek."

"And you don't mind the idea of traveling?" She flicked a gaze at Maddie, who seemed completely absorbed in her banana split.

"She has everything she needs with my mother," he replied with an edge of challenge in his voice.

He didn't have to worry. She wasn't going to challenge any decisions he made concerning his life. Even though they'd had hot sex, she had no right to challenge him about anything.

"My mother knows Red West," Melody said. "She always said Red had his hands full raising five boys and a girl on his own."

"He did a fine job," Hank replied. "The West brothers are some of the finest men I know."

"How do you know Dalton?" She spooned some of the chocolate pie into her mouth, the rich sweetness a burst of pleasure.

"We were friends as kids. Then about four years ago he worked a job in Texas not far from where my ranch was located. I don't know the details of the job, but we met in town and he became a frequent visitor to the ranch over the three months he was there. We became good friends again."

"It's nice to have friends." She spooned up another biteful of the pie, but held it halfway between her mouth and the plate as she continued. "I wish I would have taken the time to have a friend besides Lainie."

Maddie smiled at her, a ring of chocolate and strawberry ice cream around her rosebud lips. "But you have friends," she replied. "You have me and Daddy."

Melody's heart puffed up so big it filled her up. She reached across the table and grabbed Maddie's sticky little fingers. "And you're a terrific friend."

"What about Daddy? Tell him he's a good friend, too."

Melody released Maddie's hand and looked at Hank. The softness of his gaze as he smiled at her warmed her in a way she hadn't been warmed in a very long time. "And you've become a wonderful friend," she said.

Oh, but the way he was looking at her had nothing to do with friendship. Friends didn't have that flame in the depths of their eyes. Friends didn't look at each other with the hunger that radiated from his at this very moment.

"And you've become a very special friend to me," he replied, the slight gruffness in his voice sparking a familiar fire in her.

She had to take care. She knew she had to be smart, for this man and his daughter had the potential to rock her world in a way that would only lead to a new kind of heartache.

Chapter 8

"Forest Burke," Melody said into the phone the next morning. She sat at the kitchen table, a cup of coffee forgotten near her elbow. "That's who Lainie was supposed to have a date with on the night of her murder."

"How do you know that?" Zack West's deep voice boomed across the phone line.

"I had a talk last night with James O'Donnell. He told me."

There was a long pause and she could almost feel the lawman's disapproval wafting through the wire. "How would he know who Lainie had a date with that night?" he finally asked.

"He was stalking her. I think he knew more about her life than anybody realized." Melody thought about the way James had looked at *her*. Something in his eyes had made her feel dirty and violated. "Are you sure his alibi for the night of the murder is solid?"

"As solid as anyone else's. His mother insists he was home at ten and they watched a movie together until after midnight, when he went to bed."

"Is it possible his mother is lying?" Melody pressed the receiver closer to her ear. James was the best suspect they had and she couldn't believe he wasn't responsible for Lainie's death.

"Let it go, Melody," Zack said softly. "Go home and let us do our job. By involving yourself in all this you're only making things more difficult for us. I'd much rather spend my time investigating your sister's murder than having to find out who might be threatening you because you're stirring things up."

"You'll call me if you find out anything about this Forest Burke?" she asked, pointedly ignoring his unwelcome advice.

He released an audible sigh. "I'll let you know what I find out," he agreed and they disconnected.

First her mother and Fred, then an anonymous caller and now the sheriff—everyone seemed to want her to head back to Chicago. Nobody seemed to understand that Lainie had needed her in life and still needed her in death.

Melody wasn't about to go anywhere…at least not yet.

She left the kitchen and moved to the doorway of the bathroom where Lainie had breathed her last gasp. Even the morning sun streaking in through the windows couldn't banish the cold that grabbed hold of her as she stared into the room.

She hadn't entered this room since her arrival, but now it was time to face the task of packing up the items inside.

She wrapped her arms around herself and thought of Hank and Maddie, seeking anything to generate some warmth to replace the icy core inside her.

Dinner the night before had been wonderful—too wonderful. She needed to put some distance between herself and Hank. He was drawing her in too deep. But at the moment, as she faced entering the bathroom, she wished he were standing beside her, his calm, steady presence giving her the strength she needed to face the demons that lingered in the room.

"You can do this," she said aloud. "You don't need Hank here. You've never needed anyone." No one but Lainie, and she was gone forever.

She was just about to step into the room of death when a soft knock sounded at the door. A smile curved her lips. She recognized that little knock.

"Good morning," she said to Maddie as she opened the door.

"Morning," she replied. "My grandma is going to come get me in just a few minutes. As usual we're gonna spend the day together." She flopped down on the sofa. "So I thought I'd come visit you while I was waiting for her."

"I'm glad you did," Melody said as she sat beside the little girl. "What do you and your grandmother have planned for today?"

Maddie shrugged her slender shoulders. "I don't know. We might go to the movies or we might bake a cake."

"Which would you rather do?" Melody asked.

A sad frown etched across Maddie's little forehead. "I'd rather stay home with my daddy." She sighed, a sigh far too deep for one so young. "But he's always got stuff to do and wants Grandma to keep me."

"Did you sleep well last night?" Melody asked in an attempt to change the subject.

Maddie's frown didn't ease. "I had bad dreams."

Melody smiled. "It was probably those two desserts you ate last night."

Maddie tilted her head to one side and eyed Melody. "I don't think so, 'cause I have bad dreams even when I don't eat two desserts."

Melody scooted closer to the little girl. "You want to talk about the bad dreams?"

Maddie's face scrunched up with an expression of such unhappiness it resonated through Melody. "I just dream that my daddy goes away and never comes back." A tiny sob caught in her throat.

"Oh, honey, it's just bad dreams, that's all." Melody pulled Maddie into her arms, surprised when the little girl wrapped her arms around Melody's neck and eagerly accepted the embrace.

Maddie cuddled against her, her face burrowed in the crook of Melody's neck as Melody stroked her hair. "You know bad dreams are really nothing more than fears that come out in the dark."

"I don't like them," Maddie said angrily. She remained in Melody's arms for several minutes, allowing Melody to caress her thin little back.

The complete and utter trust she felt radiating from Maddie shot straight to Melody's heart, and she realized that walking away from this child would be almost as difficult as walking away from her father.

Maddie finally raised her head to look at Melody. "Lainie had nightmares, too."

"Yes, she did. But you know what always helped Lainie not be afraid?"

"What's that?" Maddie asked.

"Come with me." Melody got up from the sofa and took Maddie by the hand. She led her down the hall into Lainie's bedroom. There was only one thing left in there, the Guardian Angel picture that Melody had intended to take back to Chicago with her. But she had a feeling that Lainie wouldn't mind what she was going to do.

"See that picture on the wall?" she asked.

Maddie nodded. "That was Lainie's most favorite picture in the whole wide world."

"That's right. Lainie loved it because whenever she was afraid all she had to do was look at it and she didn't feel afraid anymore." Melody walked over to the wall and removed the picture. "And I think Lainie would like you to have it to hang in your room."

"Really?" Maddie's eyes widened and she threw herself at Melody and hugged her around the waist. "I loved Lainie and I love you, Melody," she whispered.

The words, spoken with such heart, pierced through Melody. She didn't want Maddie to love her. She was just a person passing through Maddie's life and didn't want to be the source of more heartache for the child who had already lost too much.

She knelt down in front of Maddie and gave her the

picture. "You're going to love lots of people in your life, Maddie…Madeline. And when I go back to Chicago in a couple of weeks we can write to each other, okay?"

Maddie reached out with one hand and placed it on Melody's cheek. "You can call me Maddie."

At that moment there was a louder knock at the door. Maddie dropped her hand and clutched the picture to her chest. "That'll be my dad or my grandma."

It was Susan and within minutes she and Maddie had left and Melody was once again alone to face the daunting task of clearing out the bathroom.

She leaned against the wall just outside and wrapped the memory of Maddie's sweetness around her like a shield. She had a feeling what Maddie needed most in the world at the moment was more of her daddy.

Again she tried to tell herself that it was none of her business. Soon she'd be home in Chicago and all of this would just be a dream, part nightmare and part happy memories.

Drawing a deep breath, she stepped into the bathroom and began emptying the medicine cabinet and the cupboard beneath the sink.

She packed everything she found under the sink in a box and the items in the medicine chest went into the nearby white wicker wastebasket.

She kept her mind carefully removed from what she was doing and instead focused on the little girl who had managed to crawl deep into her heart in an incredibly short period.

What she didn't want to think about was Lainie, and the last moments of her sister's life in this room. She kept a mental vision of Hank, strong as a rock and with shoulders wide enough to heft a mountain.

Blue guest towels with little gold stars and moons reminded her of Hank's eyes. Last night in the video store as she'd faced James across the counter, Hank had stood beside her like a mature tree that no wind, no act of nature or man could tumble. She'd drawn her strength from his nearness, and it scared her just a little how much she'd come to depend on him through this ordeal.

Finally, everything was sorted. She carried the boxes to the living room, then went back to get the wicker wastebasket. For a moment she stood in the center of the bathroom, and it was as if she could feel Lainie's spirit, restless and needy.

For all of Melody's life Lainie had needed her and until that need had been sated, Melody wasn't going anywhere. With a deep sigh she grabbed the wastebasket to carry it into the kitchen and empty it into the bigger trash can.

She'd just emptied it and was about to put the wicker basket into the trash as well when something blue sparked in the sunshine, something caught in the woven wicker strands.

Curious, she used a fingernail to dig the small item out. As it fell into the palm of her hand, she stared at it in confusion.

It was a shiny stone. She frowned. She'd seen something like this before. She carefully laid it on the counter and looked closely at the wicker basket, her heart freezing as she saw a splatter of blood around the area where the stone had lodged.

Excitement rocked through her as she realized that it was possible she had just found the first piece of real physical evidence.

Hank had awakened that morning in a strange panic. For in that moment between sleep and complete wakefulness, he couldn't get a mental picture of Rebecca in his head.

Every morning since the day of her death, a vision of her had been the first thing that filled his mind when he opened his eyes. But this morning it refused to come. Instead his head had filled with a picture of a different woman.

Melody.

Guilt had pulled him from the bed and into the living room, where a small photo of Rebecca rested on one of the shelves on the entertainment center. He'd picked up the photo and stared at it and had waited for the incapacitating grief to consume him. But it hadn't come.

Instead of the killing grief, only a quiet sadness had filled him for the life that had been taken far too soon. The moment his mother had taken Maddie for the day, he'd left his place and headed for the shooting range on the outskirts of town.

Emptying several clips into the targets had eased some of the restless tension that had plagued him. From the shooting range he'd gone to the café for lunch.

As he'd sat in a booth alone, he'd realized he needed to cool it with Melody. He was spending far too much time thinking about her. The sound of her laughter put a smile in his heart. Talking to her about nothing more important than the weather reminded him of what it was like to share companionship with somebody. And the dizzying scent of her perfume kept him in a slow burn of desire.

He'd stood at his wife's graveside and promised there would never be another. Rebecca had been his soul mate and he intended to honor their commitment to each other until the day he died.

He'd left the café with a determination to keep Melody at bay. He'd made the mistake of sleeping with her, of letting her get just a little too close, but he had to stop it now. Maybe if he wasn't aiding and abetting her in her private investigation she'd give it up and go back home. Then he'd fall back into the comfortable position of mourning what would never be.

As he walked down the hallway toward his town house door, he stiffened as he saw Melody leaning against the wall just outside.

Dressed in a pair of jeans and a pink sleeveless blouse with pink sandals, the sight of her stirred him and caused the resolve he'd just made to waver. Her hair was pulled into a careless ponytail that exposed her delicate features and graceful neck.

She saw him and offered a wide smile, those impossibly blue eyes of hers sparking with excitement. "I've been waiting for you! I'm so glad you're back. I have something to show you."

He wanted to tell her he was busy, that just because he'd agreed to do a little bodyguard service for her didn't mean he'd be at her beck and call anytime she wanted him. He wanted to tell her to find somebody else to talk to, but as he unlocked his door and her scent eddied in the air around her, he knew he wasn't going to do any of those things.

He hated the faint edge of joy that swept over him as she glided through the door in front of him. He hated that only moments ago he'd been planning on cutting her out of his life and now welcomed her in with a bewildering sense of pleasure.

She preceded him into the living room and stopped in the center of the room. She turned and faced him, a glow in her eyes he'd never seen before.

"You look like the proverbial cat who swallowed the canary," he observed. "What's going on?"

"I was cleaning the things out of the main bathroom and I found something." Her slender body nearly vibrated with energy.

"Found what?" Despite his intentions to the contrary, he took a step closer to her.

She pulled a small plastic bag from her pocket and handed it to him. He looked at the small blue stone inside the bag, then gazed back at her curiously.

"I found it lodged in the wicker wastebasket. There was a little bit of blood around it." She curled her fingers around his forearm, heat firing inside him at her touch. "I think it's a clue, Hank. I think the killer left it behind."

"Whoa, let's not jump to conclusions," he exclaimed, grateful when she dropped her hand from him.

"I know, I'm trying not to," she agreed. "But I've spent the last thirty minutes while I was waiting for you to get home trying to think of how it could have gotten stuck in the basket and where it might have come from.

The minute I saw it I knew I'd seen something similar before, then I remembered. It looks exactly like the stone in the college ring that Fred has."

He frowned. "Are you suggesting that Fred—"

"No, of course not," she said, cutting him off. "Fred's never been in Lainie's apartment, and I saw Fred's ring just the other day. My mother is wearing it around her neck." She rolled her eyes at his quizzical look. "Don't ask. Anyway, I think the stone is from a Maple Park College ring, and I think when the killer was beating Lainie it flew out."

Once again Hank looked at the stone in the plastic bag. It was about the size to have come from a ring. "Are you sure it isn't something that came from some piece of jewelry that belonged to your sister?"

"I'm sure. Lainie wasn't a jewelry kind of woman. She wore a single silver band on one finger, but didn't care for any other jewelry. If that's what I believe it is, then we know the killer had a ring from Maple Park and he probably attended the college."

He hated to douse the shine in her eyes, didn't want to tell her that the stone could have been lodged in that wastebasket for months. "We need to take it to Zack and let him decide what it is and if it's important to the investigation."

She nodded and began to pace on the light gray throw rug in front of the coffee table. "I'll take it to Zack, then I'm going to go out to the college to spend the afternoon looking at yearbooks. I can make a list of men I recognize from town who attended the school and maybe on that list will be our killer."

"Sounds like a plan," he agreed and consciously

didn't offer to go with her or to help. He couldn't imagine that she'd be in any danger on a college campus and she'd certainly be safe driving as far as from here to the sheriff's office. It was time to seek that distance from her, time to slowly cut her out of his life.

She took the plastic bag from him. "I'll let you know what I find out." She gave him a smile that exploded warmth in his groin. "I think we're closer, Hank. I think we're getting closer to the man who killed Lainie."

With those words she turned and left his town house. He moved to the window that looked over the parking lot. A moment later she burst into the sunshine and headed toward her car.

Her hips swung with just enough rhythm to heat his blood. Her purse was slung over her shoulder and she carried a white wicker basket he assumed had held the stone before she'd found it.

He watched her until she reached her car and slid in behind the steering wheel. He continued to watch as she pulled out of the parking space and headed out of the complex lot.

He was about to turn away from the window when he noticed another car pulling out just after her. He narrowed his gaze and focused on the driver. A small gasp escaped him. The driver looked like James O'Donnell. Hank's blood turned to ice as he raced to grab his keys. What in the hell was James O'Donnell doing following Melody?

Chapter 9

Melody pulled into the space in front of the sheriff's office, excitement winging through her. She had no illusions. Finding the killer had proven difficult so far. But surely this would help. At least it was a piece of the puzzle. It was time they finally got a break in the case.

She got out of the car and grabbed the wicker basket from the seat next to her. Her heart beat hard and fast as she approached the brick building that housed the sheriff's office.

A hand fell on her shoulder and she gasped and whirled around to see Hank. His features were set in grim determination as he grabbed her by the arm, his gaze narrowed as he eyed the street.

"Hank! What are you doing here?"

"Don't you look in your rearview mirror? Don't you

pay attention to your surroundings?" Irritation made each word bitingly short.

"What are you talking about?" she asked. She pulled her arm from his too-tight grasp.

"James O'Donnell. That's what I'm talking about." A muscle ticked in the side of his jaw. "He followed you out of the town house parking lot."

Melody swallowed a gasp of surprise. She hadn't noticed anyone following her. "What was he doing there?"

"Your guess is as good as mine, but I can promise you he had no business there and he definitely had no business following you."

She looked around the streets. "Where is he now?"

"He drove on when you pulled in here. I think he saw me in his rearview mirror." He grabbed her arm once again. "Come on, let's get inside and talk to Zack."

It was obvious he was irritated and Melody wasn't sure why his ire seemed to be directed at her. "Look, I'm here, I'm fine and James is gone. There's no reason for you to bother coming in."

"I'm coming in," he said in a tone that brooked no argument. He opened the door to the office and pulled her through as if she were a reluctant witness. "We need to speak to Zack," he said to the woman behind the front desk.

She flipped a thumb toward a nearby doorway. "He's in there." Hank knocked quickly then opened the door.

"Can we talk to you, Zack?" he asked.

Zack stood up from his desk and gestured the two of them into seats in front of him. "What's up?" He eased back down as they both sat.

Melody leaned forward and placed the wicker basket in the center of his desk. "This is from the bathroom where Lainie was killed." She explained to him about cleaning the bathroom and finding the small blue stone wedged in the wicker.

Zack took the plastic bag containing the stone from her and eyed it closely. "It's evidence, isn't it?" she asked eagerly.

"I don't know what it is," he said thoughtfully. "But I'll take it and check it out. I can't believe my deputies missed this when they went over the scene." His jaw tightened. "Since I took over as sheriff, I've discovered a lot of carelessness. Jim Ramsey didn't run a tight ship, but I'm changing things. Whoever overlooked this will answer to me."

Melody quickly told him her theory that it had come from a Maple Park College ring, that it might have shot out of the ring when the killer was beating Lainie. Zack listened patiently and promised to follow up.

Melody didn't mention that she intended to do a little follow-up on her own. She started to rise, but sat back down when Hank showed no intention of leaving.

"James O'Donnell was in the parking lot of the town houses a little while ago and followed Melody as she left," Hank said. "He seems to be as interested in Melody as he was in her sister."

"Unfortunately, I can't do anything about him just happening to be behind Melody as she drove away from her place," Zack replied. He directed his gaze to her. "This is why it's not a good idea for you to go off half-cocked asking questions."

"It's possible James was visiting somebody in the town houses and just happened to leave at the same time I did," Melody said in an attempt to ease what felt like a sudden tension between Hank and Zack.

"Yeah, and it's possible I'm going to run buck naked down Main Street at noon tomorrow," Hank returned dryly.

"I'd sell tickets to that event," Zack said with a slow smile that seemed to dispel the tension.

He leaned back in his chair and sighed, his gaze lingering on Melody. "You know, you do look a lot like your sister." He frowned thoughtfully and exchanged a dark glance with Hank. "I'll have a little chat with James."

Hank nodded. "I'd appreciate it." He stood up and Melody followed suit.

"Is it possible James's mother lied about him being home the night of Lainie's murder?" she asked.

"Anything is possible," Zack conceded. "Trust me, James O'Donnell is at the top of our suspect list. But suspecting and proving are two different things and at the moment we have nothing to prove that he's guilty. Stay away from him, Melody. My advice to you this afternoon is the same as it was this morning. Get back to your life and let us take care of the murder investigation."

"I know it's James O'Donnell," Melody said to Hank as they walked back out into the afternoon sunshine. "The man looks like a murderer." She fought a shiver as she thought of the way James had looked at her the night before in the video store.

"Do me a favor." Hank's features were stern in the

bright light of the day. "Go home. Go back to the town house and stay inside where you're safe. You've had a warning phone call and a brick thrown through your window. You've been put on notice that somebody isn't happy with you."

Melody heard the exhaustion in his words. She suddenly realized how much she'd been depending on him. No, taking advantage of him. She'd bothered him in the middle of the night, had kept him up late almost every night that they'd been together.

"Hank, I'm so sorry. I've been taking advantage of your kindness."

His features relaxed a bit. "I just think maybe it would be best if you'd keep a low profile for a day or two."

"Okay, I can do that," she agreed, her mind spinning on how she could accomplish what she wanted to from the confines of the town house.

"Good. I'll follow you back home."

Minutes later, as she drove home with Hank's car behind her, she wondered what might have happened if Hank hadn't seen James following her.

If James had been obsessed with Lainie, was it possible that obsession had been transferred to her? Would James have found a way to confront her? Would he want to hurt her as she suspected he'd hurt Lainie?

For the first time she realized the gravity of what she'd been doing. She was chasing a man who had killed before and probably wouldn't hesitate to kill again to protect himself.

She didn't intend to stop trying to hunt down the person who had taken Lainie away from her, but she knew that Hank was right. She needed to take a couple of days and keep a low profile.

While she was unwavering in her desire to catch the killer, she wasn't a complete fool. The phone call and the brick through the window told her she'd already stirred up a hornet's nest. It wouldn't hurt to let things cool down a trifle.

"Would you and Maddie like to come over for dinner tonight?" she asked Hank as they walked side by side into the building.

"Sorry, we've got plans for tonight." He paused at her doorway and again she felt a distance emanating from him.

"No problem," she said with forced lightness. "I guess I'll just see you in the next day or two." She turned to unlock her door.

"Melody, I'd really like you to take a couple days off investigating and stay inside, but if you have to go someplace, call me." The hard gleam in his eyes softened. "I don't want you running around town without your bodyguard."

"Okay. I promise at least for the rest of today and tomorrow I'll work inside."

He nodded and without another word walked down the hallway to his door. Melody entered the apartment and went directly to the window, looking for any sign of James O'Donnell lurking around. But as far as she could tell he was nowhere to be seen.

She'd intended to go to Maple Park College and look through the yearbooks for alumni. She hoped some of that work could be done by computer. Surely there was an alumni site of some kind or a message board she could check out. If worse came to worst, she'd call and order yearbooks and have them delivered to her door.

Lainie usually dated men around her own age and she figured if she ordered three or four years of yearbooks, she could at least check to see if James had attended the college.

She was surprised to discover that she dreaded the night to come—a night spent alone. Hank's subtle withdrawal rammed home the point that he was a comrade in seeking Lainie's killer, a man she'd found passion with for a single night, but nothing more.

On impulse she called her mother and invited her and Fred over for coffee that evening. "Nothing fancy," she told Rita. "Just coffee and store-bought cookies."

"That sounds wonderful," Rita exclaimed and sounded ridiculously pleased by the offer, which made Melody realize she'd been neglecting her for the past couple of days.

The afternoon flew by as Melody surfed the Web, surprised to discover that Maple Park College did, indeed, have an alumni site that was a busy place.

The message boards alone kept her busy for several hours. At dinnertime she stopped only long enough to make herself a sandwich and ate it while working on the computer. Her excitement peaked as she discovered James O'Donnell had been a student at the college. Of course, that didn't mean he'd bought a school ring.

Dean Lucas had also attended the college. But Dean Lucas hadn't looked at her with those reptilian black eyes. Dean hadn't been obsessed with Lainie to the point of Lainie talking about needing a restraining order against him.

Her next course of action would be to check the jewelry stores in town to see if anyone had brought in a class ring to be repaired. She'd talk to Hank about it tomorrow.

She shut down the computer and wondered what Hank's plans were for the evening. Had he really had something to do, someplace to go, or had he been blowing her off? Tired of his impulsive offer to play bodyguard to her? Tired of her company?

At six o'clock her mother arrived alone. "Fred sends his regrets," Rita said as she kissed Melody's cheek. "He has a strip mall on the west edge of town having a grand opening next week and some problems have come up. He had to meet with the owner this evening."

"Then it will be just us girls," Melody replied and gave her mother a hug before leading her into the kitchen.

"Have you arranged for a Realtor yet?" Rita asked once she was settled at the table and Melody had poured their coffee.

"Not yet," she admitted. "I've still got the living room and kitchen to pack up, then I figure I'll call somebody to put it on the market."

"Don't wait too long. Fred says the market here in town is hot right now, but you never know when it will cool." Rita reached for one of the cookies on a platter in the center of the table.

For the next thirty minutes they chatted about inconsequential things. Rita talked about her latest beauty shop appointment and how she didn't like the way they'd done her hair. They spoke about Rita's upcoming birthday, and as always she insisted she didn't want anyone to go to any bother about presents or a party.

"I've heard through the grapevine that you've been seeing quite a bit of Hank Tyler and his little girl," Rita said and reached for a second cookie. Although she gazed at Melody perfectly innocently, Melody felt hope radiating from her.

"Don't look at me that way. It's nothing," Melody replied hurriedly. She didn't want her mother to think there was anything there. "Hank and I have just become friendly as temporary neighbors."

The smile on Rita's face faltered slightly. "Oh, I was hoping maybe…" She allowed the rest of the sentence to trail off. "Maddie's such a little doll, and I believe the term you young people use these days for a man like Hank is that he's a hottie."

Melody laughed. "Okay, I'll admit he's hot, but seriously, we're just friends. Mom, someday I'll find my prince," she said. "But, trust me, it's not Hank Tyler. And speaking of princes, when are you going to put Fred out of his misery and marry him?"

Rita touched the ring hanging beneath her dress. "I don't know. Part of me thinks that after all this time being together, getting married is rather silly."

"But it would make Fred happy," Melody said softly. "Let me see that going-steady ring again."

Rita pulled the necklace out from beneath her dress and Melody leaned forward to get a better look at the stone in the ring.

The size, shape and color looked exactly like the stone she'd found in the basket. She told her mother about the stone she'd taken in to Zack West. "It could be a clue," she exclaimed. "It's possible it might lead us right to Lainie's killer."

"Oh, honey, why are you involving yourself in this? Go back to Chicago, Melody," Rita said and reached across the table to take Melody's hand in hers. "Go back and do your job and meet a nice man. Give me some grandkids and build a wonderful life for yourself."

"I will, Mom," Melody said. "Eventually I'll go back."

"Not eventually. Now." Rita squeezed Melody's hand. "You filled each and every one of Lainie's needs from the day you were born. Now it's time you meet your own needs."

Melody pulled her hand away from her mother's. "And I will," she agreed. She leaned back in the chair. "I can't explain it, Mom. But...I still feel Lainie all around me, and she still needs me. She needs me to help find out what happened to her."

Rita's eyes grew misty. "Sometimes in the middle of the night, I wake up and I think I hear her calling me like when she was a little girl."

"Maybe it's time you got on with your life," Melody said. "If you want to marry Fred, then for goodness' sakes, do it. You've certainly waited long enough. You can get married then come and honeymoon in Chicago and visit me."

The mist in Rita's eyes disappeared. "That would be nice, wouldn't it?" She touched the ring on the necklace around her neck and she frowned thoughtfully. "It's ridiculous, I don't know what's holding me back. Fred has been a source of support for a long time."

She leaned back in the chair and tucked the ring back beneath her dress. "I've lived alone for a lot of years—maybe I've become so set in my ways I'm not sure I'm willing to live with Fred at this point in our lives."

"I just want you to be happy," Melody said.

Rita smiled. "Funny, that's what I want for you."

Melody didn't share everything with her mother. She didn't tell her about James O'Donnell, nor did she mention that she intended to check out the jewelry stores in town.

Rita had spent a lifetime worrying about her eldest daughter, a worry that she'd no longer have because the worst of her worries had come true. Melody didn't want to become a source of further concern for her mother.

It was after eight when Melody walked her mother to the door and the two women said goodbye. "Please don't hesitate to call me if you need help here," Rita said. "Contrary to what Fred says, I'm quite capable of taking care of things. I could help with boxing up things."

"I appreciate the offer, but I'm doing fine. Within the next couple of days I should have everything done here and it will be in the hands of a Realtor."

"And then you'll get back to your own life?" Rita asked hopefully.

"We'll see how things go," Melody replied and refused to give in to the concern that darkened her mother's eyes. She laughed lightly. "I keep getting the feeling that you're trying to get rid of me."

"Of course not," Rita exclaimed hurriedly. "You know that there's nothing I'd love more than if you'd find a job here in town and stay. What I don't want is you involving yourself in Lainie's case. Leave it to Zack."

"I'm trying, Mom. I'm trying."

After Rita walked out the door Melody moved to the window where she could watch her mother get into her car. A burst of love filled her heart as she saw Rita walking across the parking lot, her blue dress whipping around her still-shapely legs in the evening breeze.

Certainly Rita hadn't expected to lose a husband so early in life, then suffer the unnatural experience of burying her child.

She watched her mother pull out of the parking lot, then started to turn away from the window but paused as she spied a man standing near a parked car.

James O'Donnell.

Her heart began a rapid banging in her chest. His gaze seemed to be intently focused on the window where she stood. She stumbled backward, her first thought to call the sheriff or Hank, but she realized there was little they could do. He wasn't breaking any laws. He wasn't threatening her.

He was just standing there…staring.

Turning away from the window, she ran to the front door and made sure it was locked with the dead bolt engaged. She leaned her back against the door, willing her heartbeat to slow to some semblance of normal. But nothing felt normal as she moved back to the window and stared at the man she believed had killed her sister.

Chapter 10

Larry Jenkins shook his head. "I've seen a ton of those class rings over the years for stone replacements. For the price the students pay for them, you'd think they could use a little extra gold and prong them properly. But I haven't seen one for about a year or so." He smiled at Hank and Melody with apology. "Sorry I can't be more help."

"That's all right. Thank you for your time," Melody said lightly, but Hank could hear the underlying disappointment in her voice.

He hadn't seen her for the past two days, not since he'd followed her to Zack's office when James had been following her. She'd called first thing that morning to see if he'd accompany her to the three jewelry stores in town.

He'd readily agreed. Over the course of the past two days it had surprised him how much he'd missed her company, had missed seeing her smile. She'd be leaving town soon enough and in the end he'd decided to enjoy her presence while she was still here.

Of course his other reason for agreeing to accompany her was that he was still concerned about her safety. While there had been no other overt or subtle threats to her over the past two days, she'd told him that she'd seen James lurking around the parking lot of the town houses.

Hank had no idea if James O'Donnell was guilty of killing Lainie or not, but he wanted to make sure that O'Donnell didn't get an opportunity to hurt Melody in any way. He'd hoped that Zack would warn the man away, but either Zack hadn't talked to him yet or James hadn't listened.

"Well, that was a bust," she said as they left Jenkins Jewelry.

"We have two more places to check before we declare the day a failure," he reminded her. As always, when they hit the sidewalk, his attention focused less on her and more on their surroundings.

The morning sun beat down on his shoulders as he gazed in first one direction then the other, seeking any potential source of danger. His gun was tucked snugly at the small of his back, the bulge hidden by his untucked dress shirt. As long as he was with Melody he wouldn't be without the gun and he wasn't afraid to use it if the situation warranted.

They headed down the sidewalk toward Raymond's Gold and Jewelry. "I got the kitchen all packed up yesterday except for the few pots and pans I'm still using," she said.

"I'll bet you're eager to get back to Chicago," he replied.

She frowned thoughtfully. "In some ways, but I love the small-town charm of Cotter Creek. I'd forgotten what it was like to wake up to birdsongs and the smell of pastures instead of the constant noise of traffic and sirens."

"I couldn't handle big-city living," Hank replied. "I hated it whenever I had to leave the ranch to go into Dallas for anything. Besides, I want Maddie to be raised in a small town without so many of the influences a bigger city offers."

She cast him a sideways glance, her eyes as blue as the T-shirt she wore. "You know it's absolutely none of my business, but Maddie seems to need more of you than you're giving her."

Hank stopped walking and stared at her in surprise, a hint of irritation rearing its head. She must have seen the irritation for she offered him a smile of apology. "I'm sorry. That was out of line."

Just that quickly Hank's ire fell away and he realized he was aggravated because he knew she was right. "Don't apologize." He drew a deep breath. "I know you're right. I think in some part of my head I've been preparing her for the time I'll be spending away from her with my new job with Wild West Protective Services."

"It's going to be hard on her without you," Melody said softly and there was something in her gaze, something soft and caring, that both drew him and repelled him. It repelled him because he realized it would be far too easy to depend on her caring.

As much as he'd loved Rebecca, as easy as it was to

cling to her memory, it was difficult to hide beneath his comfortable grief whenever Melody was around.

"She's tough," he said gruffly. "Come on, let's get to those two other jewelers before it gets too hot to be outside."

It took an hour to go to the remaining jewelry stores and discover that nobody had brought in a Maple Park College class ring needing a stone replacement in the last couple of weeks.

By the time they headed back to Hank's car, the weight of Melody's disappointment was palpable. "Want to grab some lunch before I take you home?" he asked, wishing there was some way he could alleviate her frustration.

"Okay," she replied without any real enthusiasm.

They settled in at a table toward the back of the busy café, two of many lunchtime diners. She stared at the menu for several minutes and as she did, Hank found himself staring at her.

Her long hair was pulled back and tied at the nape of her neck with a blue ribbon. Her slender neck seemed to invite the attention of his lips and he knew that behind her ears he'd find one of the sources of her evocative scent.

She looked lovely but sad. He wanted to take the sadness from her beautiful eyes, see that sunny smile of hers that always pulled an answering smile from him.

"I guess I'll just get a salad," she said as she set the menu aside. "I'm really not hungry."

"That's because you're disappointed," he observed. "You can't let this get you down."

"I know. I guess I was just hoping the killer would

be stupid enough to take his ring into one of the local shops for repair."

"You've been watching too much television," he said teasingly, then sobered. "We aren't one hundred percent positive that stone is from a ring," he reminded her.

"But I'm one hundred percent positive that I believe James O'Donnell is Lainie's killer. All I need to do is figure out a way to get close enough to him to somehow trip him up."

Fear erupted inside him. "Melody, don't," he said softly. "Don't try to get close to him. Don't talk to him anymore. If what you believe is right, then he's more than just a stalker—he's dangerous."

At that moment, with his fear for her tightening his chest, he realized that somehow she'd become more to him than a simple fling. He cared about her, and with each day that passed—with each minute he spent in her company—he cared about her more.

He was grateful when the waitress arrived to take their orders, her friendly chatter overriding his unsettling thoughts.

"I'm sorry you're so disappointed," he said a few minutes later as she picked at her salad with disinterest. "I haven't seen you smile since we left the last jewelry store."

She looked up at him, a tiny spark of humor lighting up her eyes. "I know what you could do to make me smile."

"What's that?"

"You could run down Main Street buck naked like you mentioned to Zack the other day."

He laughed. "I'd never be totally naked. Cowboys always wear their hats."

She tilted her head to one side. "But you aren't a cowboy anymore."

Funny how that statement sent a mournful rush of emotion through him. He had a memory of the wind in his face, the sun on his shoulders and a horse beneath him. The rolling pasture stretching out as far as the eye could see had been the landscape of his dreams. But it had been his choice to give up his old life and embark on a new one.

"Then, as a bodyguard, I'd have to wear my gun while I was running through the streets," he replied, pleased when she laughed.

"I can just imagine the gossip that would make its way around town. 'That Hank Tyler done lost his mind.' That's what they'd say."

He gave her a teasing grin. "Really? I was thinking that maybe what they'd be saying was that I was a fine specimen of manhood."

"That, too," she agreed.

And just that quickly there was a heat between them that would rival the griddle back in the kitchen. It sparked in the air and flooded through his veins, making his jeans uncomfortably tight.

Her cheeks brightened and she quickly averted her gaze to her salad. But even breaking eye contact with her didn't ease the hot desire that coursed through him.

He took a big swallow of his ice water, hoping to cool his thoughts—thoughts of running his hand up her sleek, long legs, of capturing the bud of her breast between his lips. He wanted that hot mouth of hers open and hungry beneath his.

"Are you about finished?" he asked, his voice deeper, heavier than usual. "I've got some things I need to take care of this afternoon." Like a cold shower, he thought ruefully.

She shoved her bowl aside. "I'm finished and I've got a full afternoon of packing still ahead of me." Her voice sounded strained as well.

The ride back home was awkward, their mutual desire a living, breathing third occupant in the car. He wanted to pull into the closest motel and take her hard and fast.

He didn't want slow and easy because he knew instinctively that would involve his heart and that was the last thing he wanted.

He'd stood at a graveside on a cold, windy February day and had vowed that his heart would never belong to another woman. His heart had been buried in a Texas cemetery, in a grave beneath an oak tree.

A sigh of relief swept through him as he pulled into his parking place. He wasn't afraid of any danger the role of bodyguard might bring his way.

He wasn't afraid of bullets or fists, or even death itself. But all of a sudden he was scared to death of Melody Thompson.

Chapter 11

"Your price is right and the place is in good condition." Mary Jane Decanter, a Realtor for Cotter Creek Real Estate, walked around the living room with a small notepad in hand. She opened the coat closet, made a note on her pad, then headed toward the kitchen.

"So you think you'll be able to sell it soon?" Melody asked, following close at her heels.

Mary Jane frowned thoughtfully. "I don't think we'll have any problems, although the tragedy that occurred here might put some people off." The frown inverted into a bright smile. "But I'm sure finding a buyer won't be a problem." Her smile turned crafty. "And you'll give me a three-month exclusive on it?"

"Sure," Melody agreed. She just wanted to get this over with. She'd spent most of the previous afternoon and all of today finishing up the last of the packing and getting the place ready to show to Mary Jane.

"The kitchen is lovely, the bedrooms are a nice size. I'm confident I can move this fairly quickly. I'll just get a contract over to you tomorrow, and once you sign it I'll get to work for you," Mary Jane said as she returned to the living room. She held out her plump hand and exchanged a firm shake with Melody. "I'll call you in the morning."

Melody nodded and saw the woman to the door. Evening shadows danced across the living room, where there was nothing left except a folding chair and a small portable television. Three men and a truck had arrived that afternoon from the local charity and had taken away all the furniture except those items in the living room and the bed Melody was sleeping on in the guest bedroom.

The last thirty minutes had been the most difficult she'd endured since Lainie's death. Once this place was sold, nothing would be left of Lainie's life except a couple of boxes of knickknacks.

If it was sold before Melody was ready to leave town, she'd either move back in with her mother or get a motel room for the duration of her stay in Cotter Creek.

She moved back to the window and stared out into the parking lot. Maybe she should put this all behind her and just head back to Chicago. Things were getting complicated here. She hadn't found out who'd killed her sister, and her mother seemed to have her own life on hold while waiting for Melody to get back to hers.

She turned away from the window with a rueful grunt. Who was she kidding? The truth was things had become painfully complicated with Hank.

Every time she saw him her heart did a crazy happy dance in her chest. Each touch between them, no matter how casual or inadvertent, caused her pulse to race with sweet anticipation. She'd vastly overestimated her ability to have a summer fling with no emotional connection.

The truth was, she was falling in love with Hank and each and every minute she spent with him only deepened her feelings.

She needed to get back to the real world, back to her cramped Chicago apartment and preparing for the school year ahead. She needed to remember that this return to Cotter Creek was temporary, as was Hank in her life.

She eased down onto the folding chair and felt the darkness of depression settling on her shoulders. Even as she thought about returning home, Lainie's voice whispered in her head.

Not yet, she said. *Don't leave me yet, Melody. I still need you. I need you to give me peace. Find my killer. Don't leave me alone in the dark. You know I hate it when night falls.*

Melody shot up off the chair and clapped her hands over her ears. What she needed was to get out of there for a little while.

There was a convenience store a few blocks away. Maybe she'd take a quick drive there and buy some ice cream. Wasn't ice cream the panacea for anything that ailed you?

She moved back to the window and scanned the area. For the past two days she'd seen no sign of James O'Donnell and she didn't see his familiar bulk lurking in the area now.

She certainly didn't want to call Hank and ask him to accompany her to pick up a gallon of ice cream. Thoughts of him were part of what she wanted to escape.

Before she could give herself time to think, she grabbed her purse and left. Shadows chased her across the parking lot to her car, but she neither saw nor heard anything to make her afraid of being alone.

The convenience store offered a vast array of comfort food and she was in the mood for a major pig-out. She realized she hadn't eaten since the day before when she'd picked at the salad with Hank at lunch. No wonder her tummy was rumbling with the need for carbs.

She grabbed a bag of cheesy corn chips, a sleeve of sinful cookies and a gallon of chocolate ice cream, then paid for her purchases and got back into her car.

Maybe when she got back she'd carry the television into the bedroom and lie in bed and eat ice cream and corn chips and watch some sobbing drama on the tube.

It was a perfect plan for a woman teetering on the edge of a broken heart, grieving the loss of a sister and mourning the additional loss of a little girl she'd already grown to love.

Night had fallen completely by the time she pulled back into her parking space. As she turned off the ignition, she realized that, during the trip from the convenience store back to the condo, she'd made the unconscious decision to remain in Cotter Creek for a while longer.

Lainie's voice would not be silent until her killer had been found and Melody still felt that somehow she was the one who needed to solve the case.

She opened her car door and grabbed her packages.

She still believed that James was the likely suspect. All she had to do was convince Zack to dig a little deeper into the man's life. What kind of a man stalked a woman who didn't want anything to do with him?

A monster.

Juggling her bags she got out of the car, the hot night air slapping her in the face and building a ravenous hunger for her ice cream. She wished she'd bought a bottle of chocolate syrup to pour over the top. She was in the mood for a double shot of chocolate comfort.

She'd gone only a few steps from the car when she was slammed from behind. Her body flew forward. She dropped her bags and purse as she threw out her arms in an attempt to break her fall.

As she crashed down, the asphalt ripped into her knees and the palms of her hands. Before the pain fully penetrated, before she could even process what had happened, a heavy boot landed a kick to her side.

Her face was smashed against the concrete with each blow. Pain crashed through her, a pain so intense she couldn't think, couldn't breathe. All she could do was curl up in a fetal ball as kick after kick smashed into her ribs.

Grunts accompanied each kick. "You were warned," a deep voice growled as she closed her eyes and begged for unconsciousness. "Get out of town. Go back where you came from."

When she opened her eyes again, all she heard was the sound of crickets in the grass nearby and a dog barking in the distance.

No grunts, no threats…just crickets and pain.

She was afraid to move but equally afraid that if she

remained where she was, somebody would find her dead in the morning.

Tentatively she rolled onto her back, nearly screaming from the pain. Her cheek was wet and warm and she raised a hand to touch it, knowing without looking that she was bleeding.

Help. She needed help. For a moment she remained unmoving, hoping that somebody would pull into the parking lot and see her, that somebody would come to her aid.

After several agonizing minutes, she realized that if she was going to get help, she needed to move. With a groan she managed to sit up, her ribs feeling as if they were broken in a hundred places.

Tears oozed down her cheeks as she tried to get to her feet. Using the side of her car as support, she eased up, the pain so intense that darkness skirted the edges of her vision.

Sucking in a breath that shot more pain through her, she began to put one foot in front of the other, focused on the door of the building in the distance.

Lainie, help me, her brain screamed. *Night has fallen and I'm scared of the dark. Someone evil found me and I'm afraid he'll find me again.*

Her mind emptied as she concentrated on getting inside the building. Each breath ripped through her, tearing her apart. Each footstep jarred her, and she had to stop after each step and fight to remain conscious.

She had to get to Hank. He'd help her. His name became a litany, a prayer in her mind as she slowly, painfully, made her way inside the building.

It felt as if it took her an eternity to make it to Hank's door. She knocked once, then slid to the floor as darkness overwhelmed her.

Hank stared at the television but his thoughts were on Melody. He'd never felt as alone as he did right now. Maddie was spending the night with his mother, and all he could think about was that he should have called Melody. She should be with him right now.

He was just about to shuck his jeans and call it an early night when he heard a knock. A glance at the clock indicated it was just after nine.

He opened the door to find nobody there. Maybe he'd just imagined the soft knock. He started to close the door when he saw her, slumped on the ground as if dead.

"Melody!" Fear rocketed through him when she didn't respond. He crouched down next to her, his gaze riveted to her bloody face as he grabbed her wrist to check for a pulse.

He nearly wept as he felt it, a faint beating that let him know that she was alive. In an instant he assessed her condition. Hands and face bloody, the knees of her jeans ripped and her complexion deadly pale.

He left her only long enough to grab his car keys and gun, then returned for her. She moaned, but didn't seem to regain consciousness as he scooped her up in his arms and carried her to his car.

Her car was parked near his and he saw her purse and a plastic shopping bag lying next to it. As gently as he could, he placed her in the backseat, sprinted over to grab her purse, then raced back to his car and slid behind the steering wheel.

Driving like a bat out of hell, he tried to stay in control, but his heart raced wildly as he all too easily imagined what had happened to her. And along with fear for her came a killing rage.

He crunched his fingers around the steering wheel, wishing he were crunching the neck of whoever had done this to her.

"It's all right, honey. You're going to be fine. We'll get you to the hospital and we'll get you fixed up." Although he had no idea if she could hear him, he babbled like a fool, hoping that on some level she'd be comforted by the sound of his voice.

Why had she gone out at night by herself? Why in the hell hadn't she called him if she needed to go out? Yet even as the question came to mind, the answer filtered through his head along with a boatload of guilt.

He could guess why she hadn't called him. For the past two days he'd been giving her all kinds of mixed signals, getting close to her then implying with a cool distance that he was tired of having her around.

Cotter Creek Memorial Hospital was a small facility, but the minute Hank pulled up in front of the emergency entrance and yelled for help, two orderlies came running out with a stretcher.

"What happened?" one of them asked as they loaded the still unconscious Melody onto the stretcher.

"I don't know. I found her like this," Hank said and hurried after them as they pushed her into the hospital. Once inside, they disappeared through a double door but a stern-faced nurse who pointed him to the waiting room stopped Hank from following them.

He walked past the waiting room and back outside where he grabbed his cell phone from his pocket and punched in the number for Zack West.

It took Zack only fifteen minutes to arrive at the hospital. He took a statement from Hank, then disappeared to find the doctor and Melody.

Hank remained in the waiting room, praying that she was okay. The hospital scent brought back bad memories. In the last weeks of Rebecca's life he'd practically lived at the hospital.

Rebecca. He was surprised that thoughts of her no longer evoked the killing grief they once had. He felt only a normal sadness for a loved one long gone.

A tall young man in a white coat came into the waiting room and Hank stood to greet him. "I'm Dr. Fedor," he said and held out a hand. "She's conscious and talking to Zack right now. But she wants to see you."

"How is she?"

"The cuts on her face and hands were superficial and she has a couple of bruised ribs, but the X-ray showed that nothing was broken. She's going to be black-and-blue for a while."

Hank clenched his hands at his sides, once again feeling a rage sweep over him. He wanted to punch somebody, he wanted someone to pay for what they'd done to Melody.

"Can I go back now?" he asked.

Dr. Fedor nodded. "She's in room three."

Hank's heart pounded as he thanked the doctor then went to see Melody. There were three examining rooms.

The first two that Hank passed were empty and a murmur of voices came from the third.

"I didn't see anyone anywhere around when I got out of my car." Melody's voice sounded weak, but thank God she was talking.

Hank entered the room and his chest squeezed tight at the sight of her. Although the doctor had told him the cut on her cheek was superficial and the blood had been cleaned off, her skin looked like it had been chewed up by grit and gravel.

Her face was unnaturally pale and her eyes, huge midnight pools, looked haunted. But as soon as she saw him, her lips curved up in a wan smile. She held out a bandaged hand to him and he quickly moved to her side and gently took it in his.

"What happened?" he asked, emotion welling up thick in his chest.

"Somebody tried to punt me over the county line," she replied.

"She was attacked," Zack said. "He hit her from behind then kicked her repeatedly."

"Who was it?" Hank asked. He tightened his grip on her hand, then quickly released it as she winced.

"I don't know. I didn't see who it was," she said, then looked back at Zack. "But if I had to make a guess, it was James O'Donnell. I think he's crazy, Zack. I think he was obsessed with Lainie and now maybe he's become obsessed with me."

Hank took several steps away from the bed and looked at Zack with narrowed eyes. "I want you to find out where James O'Donnell was tonight when this happened. If that bastard is responsible for this then you're going to have to arrest me before the night is through."

"Calm down and let me do my job," Zack said, his frustration obvious by the tautness of his features. "I'll let you know what I find out and in the meantime you keep a cool head."

Yeah, right, Hank thought angrily. Let Zack keep a cool head if his wife was beaten and left in a parking lot alone. At that moment the doctor returned and Zack left.

"I wouldn't mind keeping you overnight," he began.

Melody shook her head, that familiar stubborn glint in her eyes. "You told me nothing was broken. There's no reason for me to stay here. I want to go home."

"You're going to need some help for the next couple of days," Dr. Fedor said. "I can give you something for your pain, but you're in for a tough week or so."

"I'll take care of things," Hank said.

Dr. Fedor nodded reluctantly. "Then I'll get her discharge paperwork finished up and you can take her home."

When he once again left the room, Hank moved back to Melody's side. "Maddie didn't see me, did she?" Melody's eyes darkened with worry. "Please tell me I didn't scare her."

"No, she's at my mom's. And for the next couple of days you're going to be my houseguest."

"Oh, I couldn't do that…"

"Don't even think about declining my kind offer," he said, forcing a teasing smile to his lips.

"You have a distinct advantage over me. I'm too weak to protest," she replied.

He pulled up a chair and sat next to her. "I'm so

sorry this happened." Once again thick emotion crawled up the back of his throat. "This isn't exactly a great testament to my work as a bodyguard."

"Don't be silly. This has nothing to do with your capability as a bodyguard. You didn't know I was going out. It was stupid of me. I thought I could go just up the street without any problems. I just wanted some ice cream." Tears clung to her long dark lashes.

"Shh, don't cry. Crying will make your ribs hurt."

She laughed, then gasped with pain. "Everything makes my ribs hurt."

"I'll take you home, put you to bed and dope you up," he said.

"That's the best proposition I've heard in days." Once again she attempted a smile.

It was almost midnight by the time they left the hospital. Melody walked with slow measured steps, a gasp of pain escaping her lips with each stride. Hank wanted to pick her up in his arms and carry her, but he was afraid of hurting her even more.

"You could have been killed," he said once they were in the car and headed home.

"Yeah, I'm wondering why I wasn't," she replied.

"Maybe a car went by and spooked him or he heard something or somebody that frightened him off." He tightened his hands on the steering wheel. "All I know is that if you were a cat, you just lost one of your nine lives tonight. From here on we're not going to take a chance of you losing another one. I'm not letting you out of my sight."

"Sounds good to me," she said wearily.

By the time they got to Hank's place and he led her to his bedroom, she was beyond miserable. He helped her take off her clothes and get into one of his clean T-shirts, then tucked her into bed.

"I'll get you a couple of pain pills," he said. "I'll be right back."

As he walked into the kitchen, he thought about how right she looked in his bed, her dark hair against the white pillowcases and her warm body curled up beneath the sheets.

He got a glass of water and her pills, then carried them back into the bedroom. She swallowed two and then lay back down. "Get a good night's sleep," he said, knowing that tomorrow would be a hard day for her.

"Where are you going?" she asked, her voice already groggy.

"I'll sleep on the sofa so I don't disturb you."

"Wait, don't go." Her eyes were at half-mast and a dopey smile played on her features. "I don't want to chase you out of your own bed. Stay here with me."

"I don't want to hurt you," he protested.

"I'm too doped up to worry about that." Her smile wavered. "But I'm not so doped up that I'm still not just a little bit afraid. Stay here, Hank. Sleep beside me."

He hesitated. Reluctantly he began to undress. He laid his gun and his cell phone next to the bed and, when he was down to his briefs, he slid in beneath the sheets next to her.

She snuggled closer to him and laid one of her bandaged hands on his heart, and in that moment he knew he was in way over his head.

He was almost asleep when his cell phone rang. He reached out to grab it, grateful that the ring hadn't awakened Melody.

"Tyler," he said softly.

"It's me." Zack's deep voice chased any lingering sleepiness from Hank's head. "I just thought I'd let you know that James O'Donnell was at work at the video store when Melody was attacked. A dozen witnesses can place him there. It couldn't have been him."

"Thanks," Hank said and ended the call. Like Melody, he'd been relatively sure it had been James. If not James, then who?

Chapter 12

"We brought you flowers," Maddie said as she waltzed into Hank's room where Melody was propped up in the bed. It had been three days since her attack and, although she was starting to feel human once again, she was still stiff and sore.

The day after the attack Melody had called her mother and told her she was going out of town for a couple of days and would call when she got back. She hadn't wanted her mother to know what had happened, didn't want to worry her.

Maddie got up on the bed next to her, careful not to jiggle the mattress, and held out a fistful of daisies that looked freshly handpicked. "We saw them along the road and I made Grandma stop so I could pick you some."

"They're lovely," Melody said. "Thank you."

"Maddie, get off that bed," Susan said as she appeared in the doorway. "Melody doesn't need you wrestling around and making her ribs hurt."

"She's fine," Melody protested. "She's being very careful."

Maddie nodded. "I'm being very careful. I don't want to hurt her. She got hurt enough."

"Come on, dear, let's put those daisies in some water then we'd better scoot if we're going to make it to the movie theater on time," Susan replied.

Maddie got off the bed. "We're going to see the new movie about a little girl who raises a talking horse."

"Sounds like fun. I wish I were coming with you."

Maddie leaned over and kissed Melody on the cheek. "When you feel all better we'll go to the movies and buy popcorn and candy and have a fun time."

"It's a deal," Melody replied and smiled as Susan and Maddie disappeared from the room. She was still smiling a few minutes later when Hank came in carrying a tray with her lunch.

"I feel positively slothful being waited on like this," she exclaimed.

Hank grinned and placed the tray over her lap. "Yeah, Mom and I were just talking about that. I told her I couldn't believe what a slothful person you were."

She smacked him on the arm playfully and he dodged away with a laugh and pulled up a chair next to the bed to keep her company while she ate.

"You know, if you ever decide to get out of the bodyguard business, you'd make a pretty terrific nurse," she said. In the last two days he'd shown himself to be a patient, gentle man.

The only time she'd seen him lose his temper was when he'd helped her change the bandage around her ribs. When he'd seen the black and blue marks that had been left behind from the kicks it had taken him about two hours to calm down.

"I'm lucky that you haven't been a demanding patient," he replied.

She looked down at her lunch, a huge sandwich cut neatly in half and a mound of chips. "You make Texas-size sandwiches. I'm never going to be able to eat all this. Why don't you help me?"

"Are you sure?" She nodded and he scooted his chair closer. "Okay, if you insist."

Sleeping in the same bed for the past two nights and sharing each other's company during the days had created an easy intimacy between them.

They'd talked a lot during their confined time together. She'd shared with him the devastation of losing her father so early in life and he'd spoken a little bit about how his world was turned upside down when Rebecca had died.

Rebecca hadn't told him about the lump she'd found in her breast and she'd neglected to see a doctor. It was as if she'd believed that if she ignored it long enough it would go away. But it hadn't gone away, and by the time she'd gotten her diagnosis it had been too late. The cancer had spread.

He'd spoken at length about the ranch he'd owned. As he had, his eyes had lit with a glow that they never had when he talked about becoming a bodyguard.

Although having him close to her in the dark of the night made her feel safe and secure, it also made her yearn for something more.

Even though her ribs still hurt, the pain wasn't enough to douse her desire for him. She could smell him now, that clean, crisp scent that she would be able to identify even in the dark.

Sleeping with him at night had become a curious form of torture. He was careful to keep his distance from her, but each morning when she woke up she was spooned against him, taking in the warmth of his body and memorizing his contours.

"What are you thinking about?" he asked suddenly.

She reached for a potato chip. "Why do you think I'm thinking about anything?"

"I can see it in your eyes. There's a wicked glow there," he teased.

"That's because I'm having wicked thoughts," she replied, a breathlessness sweeping over her that had nothing to do with her bruised ribs.

He took the chip from her hand and popped it into his mouth. "How wicked are they?"

She smiled. "Very wicked. I was just wondering how fast we could lose this lunch tray so you could make love to me."

He stopped chewing mid-crunch, his eyes narrowing as he finally swallowed. "Your pain medication has obviously made you delusional."

"I'm not delusional. I'm a woman who knows what I want, and I want you." Her heartbeat raced as she waited for him to say something, to do something.

"I'll hurt you." He stared at her with such longing it cascaded warmth inside her.

"You'll be gentle," she replied, her voice a mere whisper.

He seemed frozen to the chair, then that sexy, slow grin spread across his face. "I'll be very gentle." He got up from the chair and removed the lunch tray from the bed.

A shiver of delight raised goose bumps on her skin as she watched him pull his shirt over his head. His chest gleamed bronze in the midafternoon sunshine that drifted through the window. He took off his jeans and she could see that he was already aroused.

"Are you sure?" he asked as he paused at the side of the bed. A pulse throbbed in his jaw as he looked at her.

"I've never been so sure of anything in my life," she replied. Her ribs didn't hurt half as much as her desire for him.

He eased onto the bed next to her and leaned over to take her lips with his. He held himself on his arms so that there was no other point of contact, just their mouths meeting in a hungry kiss.

Their tongues swirled and danced together and any pain that might have lingered in her disappeared beneath the intense pleasure.

Within minutes she'd pulled off her nightgown and panties and he'd taken off his briefs and their touches grew more intimate.

He leaned forward and captured the tip of one of her breasts in his mouth, his tongue teasing it to pebble hardness. The electric heat of his mouth shot directly to her groin and she moaned with a desire she'd never felt before.

"Am I hurting you?" he asked quickly and raised his head to look at her, his eyes glowing with hot intensity.

"No, it's fine. You're great," she replied huskily, just wanting him to continue.

And he did. He stroked the length of her legs, up to where she most wanted him to touch her, but denied her the ultimate pleasure of release. He touched her with only his hands and his mouth, keeping his body away from hers.

There was something incredibly erotic about the lack of skin-to-skin contact. It made each flick of his tongue, every caress of his hand that much more intense.

As his hand once again moved up her leg, lingering on her inner thigh, she reached down and took his hard length in her hand. He groaned as she stroked him and although she would have thought it impossible, he hardened even more.

With another, louder groan, he reached down and covered her hand with his, stopping her from doing any more. "You drive me crazy," he said, his eyes glowing with primeval lust. "Sleeping next to you and not touching you has made me insane."

"I know. I've felt the same way. I want you, Hank. I want you now, inside me." She didn't care about her ribs. She didn't care about anything but having this man take her over the edge, having him fill her up not only physically, but emotionally as well.

He moved away from her only long enough to get a condom from the nightstand and then he moved between her thighs, his arms on either side of her as he held his weight above her.

He entered her with a low, uneven hiss and she closed her eyes as waves of sweet sensation rippled through her. Although her ribs ached, she rose up to meet his thrusts.

As he looked down at her, his arms trembled and his features were taut. Once again, as she gazed into his eyes, she felt the kind of magic she'd once dreamed of finding with a man. As he increased his pace, she closed her eyes, losing herself to the moment, the man and the act of loving him.

She climaxed first, shudder after shudder convulsing her body as she cried out his name. He quickly followed, stiffening against her and closing his eyes.

Intense. Amazing. Magic.

"Wow," he said as he rolled onto his back next to her.

She giggled. "Wow back at you."

He propped himself up on one elbow and reached out to smooth a strand of her hair off her face. The tenderness in his eyes and in his touch suddenly filled her chest and unexpected tears sprang to her eyes.

"Did I hurt you?" His handsome face paled.

"No, not at all," she said, half laughing and half crying. "I'm fine, really. I don't know what's the matter with me."

Her reply didn't erase the stricken look from his face. "Do you need a pain pill?"

She drew a deep breath and tried to steady her erratic emotions. She hadn't had any pain medication for the last twenty-four hours, afraid that taking it any longer would create more problems than the little pills solved. "No, really I'm okay." She smiled to assure him.

"I'll be right back." He slid off the bed and disappeared into the adjoining bathroom.

Melody threw an arm across her eyes as she once again felt the press of hot tears. She'd lied to him when she'd told him she didn't know what the matter was with her. She knew exactly what caused the thick emotion that clogged the back of her throat and evoked the tears.

He hadn't hurt her by making love to her. But he was going to hurt her eventually because she'd made the incredibly stupid mistake of falling in love with Hank Tyler.

"Are you sure you're ready for this?" Hank asked as he led Melody to the folding chair in Lainie's living room. "You know you can stay at my place for as long as you want."

"Thanks for the offer, but it's time I got out of your life and back into my own," she replied. "Besides, Mary Jane is showing the place at noon today and I want to be here."

He frowned and looked around the empty room. "You can't be comfortable here. Other than that chair you're sitting on there's no furniture."

"I still have my bed in the bedroom and that's really all I need."

There was a part of him that was almost relieved that she had awakened that morning and insisted she wanted to return here.

She had gotten too close. She'd made him remember laughter and shared morning coffee and secrets whispered in the night. She'd made him remember all the things he'd loved about being married, about sharing his life.

"I'll be fine here, Hank," she said, breaking into his thoughts. "And I'll never be able to repay you for your kindness."

She'd been distant since waking up but now her eyes shone with an emotion that looked like caring, one that looked like love. It was there only a moment then gone and she quickly gave him a bright, but brittle, smile.

He shoved his hands into his pockets and moved toward the front door, oddly reluctant to leave her. "You have enough food? You need me to go to the grocery store for you?"

"I should be fine. Besides, I'm feeling much better." She rubbed her hands together as if to prove they were no longer sore. Her cheek wound was healing nicely and would leave no scar. "I can even laugh now without my ribs hurting."

He smiled but the gesture did nothing to ease a crazy little pain inside him. This felt like goodbye. Something had changed between them after their lovemaking the night before.

He should be glad that she wanted to get out of his life, that the intimacy they'd shared over the past couple of days hadn't made her believe they had a future together. But *glad* wasn't in his heart at the moment.

"Does Mary Jane think she'll be able to move this place quickly?" he asked.

"According to her, these units are highly desirable places to live. I don't think it will take her long to sell it."

And then she'd go back to Chicago. Eventually she'd fall in love and build a life with some lucky man. Strange how this thought shot a tiny shard of pain through him. But that's what he wanted for her—happiness and love—and he wasn't the man to give her those. Nor had she given him any real sign that she wanted him to be that man.

"You'll call me if you need anything?" he asked as he edged toward the door. She nodded, and for just a moment her eyes were filled with an incredible sadness.

"Are you sure you're okay?" he asked.

"Yeah." She drew a deep breath. "I was just thinking that once this place sells my last link with Lainie will be broken."

"That's not true," he replied. "You'll always have your memories of her."

This time her smile was beatific. "And they are such wonderful memories." Her smile faltered. "I just wish the person who took her from me was behind bars."

"Contrary to the television shows we watch, murders aren't usually solved overnight," he said. "It might be months before Zack has the guilty party in jail."

"Not if I have anything to say about it," she replied with a fierceness that caused his heart to plummet.

"What are you talking about?" He stepped away from the door and closer to where she sat.

"Even though James wasn't the person who attacked me in the parking lot, that doesn't mean he isn't Lainie's killer. I want to talk to his mother, find out if she lied for her son on the night of the murder. I also want to talk to Forest Burke and find out why he didn't take Lainie out that night."

Hank's blood went cold as he stared at her in disbelief. "Are you crazy? Wasn't the beating you took the other night enough for you?"

"Of course it was frightening and horrible, but I just need to be smarter and make sure I'm not out alone after dark," she replied.

"For the last couple of days and nights you haven't mentioned any more nonsense about doing your own investigating. I figured you'd come to your senses," he said flatly.

"I never lost my senses." There was a definite coolness in her voice and a hot fire in her eyes.

"What you need to do is stop it," he exclaimed. "You need to leave it alone, Melody, before you get killed."

"I can't leave it alone," she retorted as she rose from the chair. "Lainie needed me while she was alive and she still needs me to find her killer."

He rocked back on his heels, anger rising inside him. He stared at her for a long moment, trying to temper his words, but was unsuccessful and instead just let his thoughts rip out of his mouth. "You know what I think? I think it was never about Lainie's needs. I think it's always been about *your* needs. You needed her and now that she's gone you're clinging to her because you're afraid to face your own life."

He wasn't sure where the words had come from, but they felt right falling from his mouth. Throughout the last couple of days he'd heard plenty about her relationship with her sister and he knew the fancy term *code-pendent* definitely applied.

The fact that she'd been beaten and could have died was bad enough. The fact that she didn't intend to stop both terrified and enraged him.

"I think you've said enough," she exclaimed, a warning light shining from her eyes.

He was angry and reckless. The anger was a clean, uncomplicated emotion compared to his feelings for her, and he embraced it. "Dammit, Melody, go home. Go back to Chicago and forget all this. Let Zack catch the killer."

Her chest heaved and she stalked up directly in front of him. "Nobody decides when it's time for me to go back to Chicago except me." She poked him in the chest with two fingers. "And that includes you."

He grabbed her hand in his. "You're on a fool's mission and I can't be a part of your madness any longer."

She jerked her hand from his. "Then don't."

Shrugging his shoulders, he once again shoved his hands into his pockets and headed for the door. "Okay then, you're on your own."

He hoped that his bowing out would make her come to her senses and stop pursuing things that could only get her hurt. Dammit, what he wanted to do was tie her to his bedposts until she had a plane ticket back to Chicago in her hand.

"You have to let go of the grief and get on with your life," he said. As much as he'd hate to tell her goodbye, he knew with a gut-burning certainty that at the moment she was bent on a course of disaster.

He opened the door with every intention of barreling out of it and out of her life, but he paused as she called after him.

"Hank Tyler, you stop right there. You've said your piece and now I'm about to say mine," she exclaimed.

Chapter 13

Melody was mad enough to spit. Who did he think he was to say the things he had, then just waltz out the door? "If we're talking truths here, then let me tell you what I think," she began.

He slammed the door with his heel and faced her, those blue eyes of his filled with confrontation. "And what would that be?"

"I think you have a lot of nerve telling me I need to let go of my grief. I've had less than a month to mourn for my sister. You've had over two years to mourn your wife and get on with your life, but you seem hell-bent on punishing yourself, denying yourself any chance at happiness."

"You don't know what you're talking about," he said, but she saw that her words had hit a sore place by the tightening of his facial features.

Thick emotion pressed against her chest, making her ribs ache as much as her heart. Tears misted her vision but she refused to let her tears or the love she had for him keep her silent.

"I'll tell you what I do know," she said, her voice trembling. "I know that you're a cowboy...a rancher. Every time you talk about the ranch you owned, your eyes light up and you smile from your heart. I don't know why you've chosen the path you've taken to become a bodyguard, but if anyone is flirting with disaster, it's you."

"I can take care of myself," he scoffed.

Melody drew a deep breath, recognizing that the next words she intended to say would cross a line from which there would probably be no going back. But, if she could accomplish only one thing while she was here, this would be her choice for the child she'd grown to love.

"Yes, you can take care of yourself and you're doing a damn fine selfish job of it."

His eyes narrowed to dark blue slits and knotted muscles formed in his jaw. "What are you talking about?"

"You're taking a job that in a worst-case scenario might see you dead and in the best-case scenario will see you weeks away from your home...away from your daughter. She needs you, Hank. Did you know she has nightmares? Nightmares about you going away and never coming back?"

His face paled but his features remained taut and unyielding. "All kids have nightmares."

"About monsters...about ghosts, but not about daddies who go away and never come back," she exclaimed. "You've wrapped your grief around you so tightly you've made not only yourself but your daughter a prisoner of it. I'm sure that's not what Rebecca would have wanted for either of you."

"Are you through?" he asked, his voice tightly controlled and cool.

No, she wasn't through. She wanted to throw herself into his arms, tell him she loved him. She wanted to ask him to take a chance with her, to seek the magic that she knew they could find together if he'd just trust in it.

Instead she wrapped her arms around her aching ribs and nodded. "I'm through."

He whirled on his heels and went out the door without saying another word. She stared after him for several moments, a wash of tears making the wooden door wave and dance.

The silence that followed echoed in every chamber of her heart. She reached inside for anger, needing it to staunch her tears. Damn him. Damn him for not understanding. Damn him for speaking things she didn't want to hear, for confronting her with hard truths she hadn't wanted to face.

But more than anything, damn him for making her fall in love with him. More tears cascaded down her cheeks and a sob welled up, begging to be released. She swallowed hard, refusing to cry for him.

She glanced at her watch and realized Mary Jane would be there with potential buyers in half an hour. Good, because Melody desperately needed a distraction from her thoughts. Even if the people who looked today didn't buy, it was time for her to leave. All she had to do was decide if she wanted to return to her mother's house or get a motel room until she decided to go back to Chicago.

Mary Jane was on time and brought with her an older married couple whose children were grown. "We like the idea of no yard work or maintenance," Sarah Hunter said as she held tight to her husband's arm. She smiled up at him, her love obvious. "We're at a place in our lives where we'd like to do a little traveling, but we need a home base."

Sam Hunter patted his wife's hand and returned her look of affection. "For the last thirty-five years, anyplace you are is home, darlin'," he exclaimed.

As they disappeared down the hall to look at the bedrooms, Melody leaned against the kitchen counter and released a deep sigh. It was obvious Sarah and Sam Hunter were just as in love with each other today as they had probably been on the day they had married.

For thirty-five years the Hunters had shared their lives and Melody had scarcely gotten a day of loving Hank before all hell had broken loose.

I think it was never about Lainie's needs. I think it's always been about your needs. Hank's words whirled around and around in her head. She was grateful when Sam, Sarah and Mary Jane returned to the kitchen and took her away from her troubling thoughts.

"I'll be in touch," Mary Jane said as Melody led them to the front door.

Melody closed the door after them and leaned against it weakly. All she wanted to do was get into bed and pull the covers up over her head. She'd never felt so weary. The weariness of heartbreak, she thought.

Maybe a nap was just what she needed. Although her ribs were healing, she still wasn't totally up to par. Besides, in sleep she wouldn't think about the hurtful words she'd exchanged with Hank.

She went into the bedroom and took off her jeans, then, clad only in her underwear and T-shirt, she crawled beneath the sheets on the bed. She lay on her back and stared up at the ceiling, wondering what had possessed her to get involved with Hank in the first place.

Throwing herself at him sexually had been out of character, seeking his comfort and company had been equally unlike her. She tried to tell herself her attraction to him had been driven by loneliness and grief, but she didn't believe that.

Physically she'd been drawn to him by some mysterious force of hormones or whatever power had brought lovers together throughout history. Emotionally it had been his steady strength, his sense of humor and the gentleness she'd sensed inside him that had drawn her in.

It didn't matter now. None of it mattered. All she wanted was the oblivion of sleep to take away the pain inside her.

She must have fallen asleep, for the ringing of the phone awakened her. Groggily she reached for the phone, at the same time checking the clock on the nightstand. It was after four. She must have been asleep for nearly two hours.

"Hello?"

"Ah, good. You're finally home," Fred said.

For a moment she didn't know what he was talking about. Then she remembered that she'd told her mother she was visiting an old high school friend out of town for the last couple of days.

"Yes, I got back in today." She pulled herself up to a sitting position in an attempt to slough off the last of her sleep.

"Did you have a nice visit with your friend?" he asked.

"It was okay. Is anything wrong, Fred? Is my mother all right?"

"She's fine. Why?"

"I think the last time you called me was when you told me Mom was about to go into surgery to have her gallbladder removed."

Fred laughed. "Nothing like that with this phone call. I was just wondering if you'd have some time this evening to come over and help me with some plans for a surprise birthday party for your mother."

"I'm really tired, Fred. Can we make it another time?" she asked. She had no desire to go out in the evening hours, especially now that she'd lost her bodyguard. The last time she'd left to go out into the night, she'd wound up being kicked half to death.

"What about tomorrow? Why don't you come for brunch? I've been itching to make some of those apple crepes that you love."

It had been Lainie who had loved Fred's apple crepes, not Melody, but she didn't have the heart to remind him. Surely it would be safe for her to leave the building in the light of day, she thought. "Brunch sounds perfect," she agreed.

"Shall we say around ten?"

"Sounds great. I'll be there," she agreed.

After they hung up she tried to talk herself into getting out of bed, doing something constructive. She could get the phone book and hunt up Forest Burke's number. She could call Zack and get an update. What she did instead was curl up on her side, hug her pillow to her chest and fall back asleep.

Because she went to bed so early she awakened the next morning before dawn. She lay in the quiet darkness of the room and found herself contemplating what Hank had said to her.

Was she desperate to continue her search for Lainie's killer because she was afraid to let go? Afraid to face the emptiness of her life?

Had she used Lainie as an excuse not to make her own friends and explore new relationships? As much as she hated to admit it, she thought that might be true. She'd encouraged Lainie to lean on her, to need her because of her own needs. Melody was afraid of the dark, when night fell and monsters crept out of closets.

Hank's words washed over her in wave after wave of recognition. It was time for her to finally let go. No matter who she spoke to, no matter what information she gathered, it wouldn't bring Lainie back.

Hank had been right. It was time for her to go back to Chicago. She'd wait until next week after her mother's birthday, then she'd get on a plane with only her memories of Lainie and Hank and Maddie to keep her company.

It was just after nine when she heard a tiny knock on her front door. Maddie. Her heart squeezed as she thought of the child who had taken such a large chunk of her heart.

"I came to visit," Maddie said as she swept past Melody and into the nearly empty living room. She sat cross-legged on the floor in front of the folding chair. "It was more fun to visit with you when you were at my house."

"I couldn't stay there forever," Melody said as she sat in the chair.

"Why not?" Maddie looked at her with childish longing. "Why couldn't you marry my daddy and stay forever?"

Could the pain get any deeper? Melody wondered. "Because I have to get back to my life in Chicago," Melody replied, unsure how else to answer.

Maddie's lower lip punched out in a pout. "I hate Chicago," she exclaimed. At the moment Melody wasn't thrilled with the idea of returning there either.

For the next few minutes the two talked about school and summer plans, then Melody stood up. "You're going to have to leave, sweetie," she said. "I've got to go have brunch with Fred."

"Who's Fred? Is he your new boyfriend?"

Melody smiled as she walked with Maddie to the door. "No, he's the man who's going to eventually marry my mother, and that will make him my stepfather."

Maddie gazed at her with somber eyes. "So you're going to get a new daddy. I wish my daddy would get me a new mommy." She slipped her hand into Melody's. "I would have liked you as my new mommy."

Melody knelt in front of her. "I would have loved to be your new mommy," she said. "But sometimes things just don't work out the way we want them to. Maybe someday your daddy will find a special woman to be your new mommy." She leaned forward and embraced Maddie and wondered how many more ways her heart could break.

Hank was in a foul mood. The gray storm clouds gathering in the distance reflected the tumult of his thoughts. He stood at the window where he'd kept vigil the day before and sipped his coffee. After the fight with Melody he'd stormed home not fit for human company. He'd spent most of the rest of the day watching from the window that looked out on the parking lot to make sure that Melody didn't take off to do anything crazy, but her car had remained parked.

The minute he'd rolled out of bed he'd returned to the window, relieved that her car was still in the same place. He'd told her he was through playing bodyguard to a woman who intentionally wanted to stir up a hornet's nest. Unfortunately, he also couldn't stand the idea of her going off half-cocked and getting hurt again.

He drained his coffee cup and headed toward the kitchen for a fresh cup. He set down his cup and leaned against the counter, rubbing eyes gritty from lack of sleep.

It was hard to sleep with a woman's voice echoing in your head. And it was damned irritating when the words the woman was speaking held more than a grain of hard truth.

He filled his coffee cup and sat at the kitchen table where the morning paper was still wrapped in plastic in case rain fell. He was about to open it when he heard the front door open and the sound of his daughter's footsteps running toward the kitchen.

She needs you, Hank. Melody's words banged around in his brain, bringing with them a shard of pain that nearly doubled him over. She needed him and he'd let her down.

Maddie marched into the kitchen and straight to the refrigerator. "Hi, Daddy," she said as she pulled out the gallon of milk.

"Before you pour yourself a glass of milk, I want you to come here."

Maddie set the milk jug on the table and eyed him suspiciously. "Am I in trouble?"

He smiled, love for her burgeoning in his heart. "Should you be in trouble?"

"I don't think so," she said hesitantly. "But I stopped and saw Melody on my way from Grandma's house."

"Why don't you come over here and see me. I can't remember the last time I gave my best girl a kiss." The eager expression on Maddie's face as she ran to his open arms once again made his heart ache. He pulled her up on his lap, closed his eyes and relished the hug they shared.

"I love you, Daddy," she whispered against his neck.

"And I love you, baby," he replied, surprised by a sting of tears in his eyes. "And things are going to change around here."

Maddie got down from his lap and looked at him curiously. "What's going to change?"

He smiled at her, his heart suddenly lighter, brighter than it had been in years. "From now on you're going to be spending less time with Grandma and more time with me."

"That's good," Maddie said happily. "And are we gonna live on a ranch? Couldn't you be a cowboy again?"

I know that you're a cowboy...a rancher. Melody's voice once again whispered in his head.

"I don't know," he answered Maddie truthfully. "I need to think about a lot of things before I make any decisions."

"I'm gonna make me a bowl of cereal, and while I eat I could help you make the decisions," Maddie replied.

Hank laughed. "Unfortunately, this is a decision I need to make on my own." He was surprised to discover that the idea of another ranch filled him with excitement instead of the grief he'd once felt when contemplating life on a ranch.

Melody had been right about several things. He didn't want to be a bodyguard. He wanted to get back to the land where he belonged.

He had been punishing himself in some kind of crazy survivor-guilt way by selling off the ranch and choosing a job that would never make him truly happy. And he wasn't the only one who had been paying for his bad decisions. Maddie had paid as well.

"How was Melody this morning?" he asked. The anger that had driven him out of Lainie's place the day before was gone, replaced by a wistful sense of loss.

"She was good. She was leaving to go have breakfast with Fred. He's gonna be her new stepdaddy." Maddie carefully poured a mound of cereal into a bowl.

She should be safe going to Fred's, Hank thought. It

was daytime and there would be people out and about. There was no reason for him to be concerned. He reached for the morning paper and pulled off the plastic wrap.

"Daddy?" Maddie sidled up next to him. "Someday maybe could you get me a stepmommy?"

Instantly a vision of Melody filled his head. He saw her brushing Maddie's hair and laughing in delight at something Maddie had said. She would be a good mother someday, but she'd told him from the very beginning she was just in Cotter Creek long enough to find her sister's killer.

She had no interest in a long-term relationship. He'd been nothing more to her than a summer fling, a salve against the wound of loss that Lainie's murder had left behind.

"Daddy?"

Maddie's voice pulled him out of his thoughts and he forced a smile as he realized she was waiting for an answer to her question. "I don't know. Maybe someday," he replied and was pleased that she seemed satisfied with that.

As Maddie focused on her cereal, Hank pulled the paper in front of him and opened it. Splashed across the front page was a huge photo of Fred Morrison and a construction worker in a hard hat. The headline read: Strip Mall Grand Opening in a Week.

"I've seen him before," Maddie said as she looked at the picture.

"Who?"

She stabbed a little finger at Fred's face. "I've seen him before."

Hank frowned. "That's the man who's going to be Melody's stepdaddy. Where have you seen him?"

"At Lainie's."

Hank stared at his daughter in confusion. "You must be mistaken. Fred has never been to Lainie's place."

"Yes, he has," Maddie contradicted. "I saw him one night when I was coming here from Grandma's. He knocked on her door and she let him in."

Hank stared at her, his mind racing. He was sure Melody had told him Fred had never been inside Lainie's place. A faint chill strolled up his spine. Why would Fred lie about something like that?

Chapter 14

Fred Morrison's home was located at the north edge of Cotter Creek on ten acres of prime pasture, but there was nothing remotely farmlike about the house itself.

It was a huge three-story house that shouted money and success. It had always intrigued Melody that a single man could live alone in such opulence.

There was a part of her that admired the fact that her mother hadn't been seduced by the financial aspects of marrying Fred. It would have been easy for the single mother of two young girls to give in to Fred and have financial security, but Rita hadn't succumbed to the easy route.

Melody pulled her car around the circle drive and parked in front of the massive double doors. She hoped Fred wasn't planning anything elaborate for her mother's birthday. Rita wasn't one for grandiose gestures and would prefer a quiet dinner as a celebration.

The storm clouds that had been in the distance earlier had moved overhead, hanging low and dark and ominous.

Fred answered her knock. Clad in a white apron he offered her a bright smile as he gestured her inside. "Hope you brought your appetite," he said. "I've been working in the kitchen since dawn."

"And something smells wonderful," she exclaimed. "But you really didn't have to go to all this trouble."

"Nonsense, I love to cook whenever I get the opportunity. I keep telling your mother if she marries me she'll never have to cook again." Together they walked toward the back of the house where the kitchen was located.

As they passed one of the rooms, Mike the painter poked his head out and waved with a friendly smile. "Hey, Melody, how you doing?"

"Mike is working in my office," Fred explained. "After we eat I'll show you what's being done in there."

The kitchen was a large room with a cozy eat-in alcove. He motioned her to the table, which was set with attractive blue-patterned plates. Orange juice was already in the glasses and Melody sat down and took a sip.

"What happened to your cheek?" he asked as he headed toward the oven.

"Oh, it's nothing. I just scraped it when I was moving some things." She reached up self-consciously and touched the nearly healed wound.

"I realized after I spoke to you that it was Lainie who loved my apple crepes and you preferred my apple-cinnamon muffins, so I changed my menu plan." Fred opened the oven door and bent to look inside, then closed it with a frown. "And it's going to be a few minutes still before the muffins are done."

"You mentioned you were planning something for Mom's birthday? We could talk about that while we wait," she suggested.

He joined her at the table and she noticed his sleek silver cane was nowhere to be seen. She'd never known for sure why he used it, suspected that it was more for ornament than need.

"I was thinking maybe something in the back garden here." He pointed out the window to the gardens in the distance. "We could have it catered, something simple but elegant. Perhaps about fifty or seventy-five guests."

Melody laughed. "Fred, my mother doesn't know that many people." She sobered. "And given what's happened in the past couple of weeks I don't really think she'll be up for a big party."

Fred frowned. "Given what's happened, I think a big party is exactly what she needs," he countered. "She's spent a lifetime worrying about Lainie and now she doesn't have to worry anymore."

Melody sat back in her seat and stared at him. She'd never known Fred to be so insensitive before. He smiled apologetically, as if reading her thoughts. "I'm sorry, I didn't mean that the way it sounded. But you know how trying Lainie could be and all she was talking about before her death was having a baby. God, what a nightmare that would have been."

A faint alarm of apprehension went off in Melody's head. She told herself not to be ridiculous, that this was

Fred…Fred! The man who had been in their lives for years, the man who loved her mother to distraction.

"Come on, let me show you what Mike's doing in my office. We have a few more minutes before the muffins are finished."

She shoved away the crazy disquiet and stood to follow him out of the room. She was just on edge, spooked because this was the first time she'd been out since her attack.

Fred's office was a large room with a stone fireplace at one end and an ornate mahogany desk in front of it. The floor was covered with drop cloths and Mike lowered a paintbrush as they entered.

"As you can see, I'm having that beige wall painted a deep burgundy. Then I've ordered two wingback chairs to go in front of the fireplace, and we'll move the desk over there." He pointed to the other side of the room. "I wanted to pretty up the room a bit for when your mother moves in."

Melody nodded, although she found it odd that Mike would have drop cloths covering the entire floor for painting a single wall. Mike set his paintbrush down and wiped his hands on his apron and exchanged a look with Fred.

Fred looked at Melody, and in the depths of his eyes she thought she saw regret. Regret for what? Her heart banged against her bruised ribs as a sudden fear overtook her. Stop it, she told herself and drew a deep breath. There was nothing to be afraid of here.

"Melody, Melody, Melody," Fred said in a singsong

fashion. "You've become as big a problem as your sister was."

It was then she noticed the knife Mike was holding in his hand.

He was overreacting. Once again Hank stood at the window overlooking the parking lot from where Melody's car was gone. She'll be fine at Fred's, he told himself. There was absolutely no reason for his gut to be churning with anxiety.

Why had Fred told Melody he'd never been inside Lainie's place? What possible motive could he have to lie about such a simple thing?

He'd spent several minutes trying to pin down Maddie on when she'd seen Fred, but all she knew was that it was around the time that Lainie had died. Had it been on the night that Lainie had been murdered?

Why would Fred have gone to Lainie's and why would he lie about it? It just didn't make sense, and what didn't make sense made him nervous.

He jerked away from the window and slid a hand through his hair as if the gesture would help him make sense of things. Why would Fred want to hurt Lainie? The man had been like a father to her. Lainie had loved Fred. It just didn't make sense to suspect Fred of any wrongdoing.

Still, no amount of rationalization vanquished the bad feeling he had in his gut. He paced the living room, his mind racing in a million directions. Why had Fred lied?

He glanced at his watch. Ten-thirty. How long could it take Melody to eat breakfast and come back home?

He suddenly had a need to see her, to make sure she was all right.

He pulled his cell phone from his pocket and dialed his mother's phone. "Mom, I know you didn't intend to keep Maddie today, but is it possible you could watch her right now for a little while?"

"What's wrong?" Susan asked.

"What makes you think anything is wrong?" he asked.

"I'm your mother, Hank. I can hear it in your voice. Now, tell me what's wrong."

He sighed. "Probably nothing, but I need to find Melody. She went to have breakfast with Fred Morrison. I don't know why, but I just need to check on her and make sure she's all right."

"I'll be right there." Susan clicked off before Hank had fully finished speaking.

What had begun as a little whisper of worry now quickly became an urgent scream inside his head. Once his mother arrived, he grabbed his keys and headed for his car, telling himself that he was probably playing the fool, but not caring. It was at that moment that he recognized the depths of his love for Melody Thompson.

"Fred? What's going on?" Melody asked, her voice sounding tinny and small, drowned out by the banging of her heart.

"If you'd just come back for the funeral then left again nothing would have happened, but you had to dig and dig and put your nose where it didn't belong. I tried to warn you with the phone call and the brick. I told you to go back to Chicago."

She stared at him as if seeing him for the very first time. His neatly cut salt-and-pepper hair looked the same way it always had, but his handsome features were suddenly alien as his eyes radiated a weary resignation. "You?" The single word escaped her lips on a faint sigh.

"I even had Mike here rough you up, figuring that would be enough to send you packing, but it didn't." Fred walked over to the corner and grabbed the solid silver cane with the ornate head. When he looked at Melody again, his eyes were hard pellets. "She was going to get pregnant. If that happened, your mother would have never married me. She would have been saddled with raising a kid because we all know Lainie wasn't capable of being a real mother."

"You killed her?" Melody's world tilted and a new grief for her sister welled up inside her. It was bad enough for Lainie to have been killed by a stranger, but she'd loved Fred and she'd thought Fred loved her.

"I didn't intend to kill her. I went over there to try to talk some sense into her. I wanted her to get a hysterectomy so she wouldn't have any babies." Fred's eyes flashed with anger. "If she'd just done what I asked there wouldn't have been any problems, but instead she laughed at me, told me that I couldn't do anything to stop her from having a kid or two."

Melody listened in horror. She shot a glance at Mike, who stood nearby as if awaiting orders. He didn't look shocked by Fred's words. He looked bored.

"She went into the bathroom and I followed her." Fred's fingers tightened on the top of his cane. "I was in love with your mother long before your father died.

When he had his heart attack and died, I was determined that she'd be mine. I built my company for her. I built this house for her and I waited for her to finally agree to marry me. But over and over again she put me off, telling me we'd have time for our life when Lainie got settled. Lainie was never going to get settled," he screamed.

Melody took a step backward, still reeling from what she was hearing. She'd thought that the killer was James O'Donnell because he had a sick obsession for Lainie, but instead it had been Fred because of his sick obsession with her mother.

Even as she listened to him and kept Mike in her peripheral vision, she frantically looked for a way to escape. But Fred was standing by the door to the room and Mike was on her right side, in front of the windows.

"It was a tragic accident," Fred continued. "When she laughed at me I struck her—" he raised his cane and slashed it through the air and at the same time a low rumble of thunder rattled the windows "—she fell and laughed and I hit her again…and again…and again."

"And you lost the stone out from your ring," Melody said with horror.

"A trip to a jeweler in Oklahoma City took care of that problem, and I thought everything was fine, but you keep digging and digging."

"I'll stop. I'll go home and never tell anyone what you've told me," she lied.

Fred shook his head and every muscle in her body tightened as Mike took a step toward her. "I'm afraid it's too late for that. I've been a patient man, Melody, but my patience has finally run out. Mike is going to see to it that you never tell anyone anything. You're going to disappear. Your mother will go through a grieving process, but then there will be nothing more keeping her from me."

"You'll never get away with this," Melody exclaimed. "Several people knew where I was going this morning."

"And you arrived and we had a lovely breakfast together and planned your mother's birthday party, and then you left. Mike will make sure your car isn't found for months and you'll become part of the concrete foundation of a new building we're working on. People will search for you and your disappearance will remain a mystery for years to come."

He stepped backward toward the door to leave and nodded to Mike. Melody suddenly realized why the floor was covered with drop cloths. It was so there wouldn't be any mess when Mike killed her. Her bloody, dead body would be wrapped in one of those cloths and she'd be dropped into a hole and covered with concrete.

"Please," she said to Mike as Fred left the room. "How can you do this for him?"

"He pays me well for helping him out," Mike said as he advanced on her. Lightning flashed and thunder exploded. Melody raced for the door that Fred had just exited, but when she twisted the knob, it was locked.

She whirled back around and grabbed a lamp from a nearby table and held it out in front of her in an attempt to keep Mike away.

All she could think about was Hank and Maddie and her mother. They would never know what happened to her. Maddie would never get a letter from Chicago and her mother would marry the man who had murdered her two children. And Hank…he would never know that she'd loved him. He would never know that for her, he'd been magic.

The rain slowed him down. It fell in torrents, the windshield wipers barely able to keep up. Lightning split the skies and thunder boomed almost instantaneously.

But the storm outside had nothing on the tornado of emotions that was whirling through Hank. As he drove he kept telling himself that he was overreacting, that he was going to arrive at Fred's place and find Melody eating a bowl of fruit and a muffin. Hank would be embarrassed by intruding, but at least he'd have the peace of mind to know Melody was okay.

As he pulled up in the driveway, he saw her rental car in front of the door, but even the familiar sight couldn't stanch the feeling that she might be in danger.

Thankfully the rain had eased off to a mist as he got out of his car. He started for the front door, then paused and changed his mind. With the faint alarm of danger ringing in his ears, he went around the side of the house, deciding to see what he could find by peering into windows.

The alarm that had been faintly ringing in his ears became more shrill as he saw a covered pickup truck parked in the grass by a back door. Why would a worker park back here instead of in the driveway?

He crouched down and went to the first window. A peek in showed him the kitchen, but there was nobody inside. The table was set but it didn't appear that anyone had eaten yet. He frowned. She'd been here long enough to eat a three-course meal and be on her way back home.

He moved to the next window and cursed inwardly as the tightly drawn blind prevented him from seeing in. Where was she? Another rumble of thunder boomed overhead, but it sounded no louder than his beating heart.

When he looked into the next window his heart stopped. She was there—and as he watched, a man he'd never seen before rushed her with a knife.

He heard her scream as he launched himself at the window. He didn't feel the slashing glass as he broke through. He landed on the floor inside, pulled his gun and stood at the same time.

Melody was on the ground, her eyes closed as blood oozed from a wound in her chest to darken her yellow T-shirt. Hank faced the man with the knife, rage cascading red before his eyes. His fingers itched to pull the trigger. God, he wanted the man dead.

Emotions ripped through him. Was Melody dead? "Put the knife down before I put a bullet through your heart," he said.

"It wasn't my deal," the man said quickly, his eyes frantically searching for an escape route. "It was Fred. He made me do it."

Hank kept the gun trained on him while he pulled his cell phone from his pocket. "Zack, I need you out at the Morrison place. Melody has been stabbed and I just shot a man." He clicked off the phone as the man's eyes widened.

"Hey, wait!" he said just before Hank pulled the trigger. The bullet struck him mid-thigh, and with a squeal of pain he fell to the ground and writhed in pain. Hank rushed to Melody's side while keeping an eye out for Fred.

"Melody? Melody, open your eyes, honey." He used one hand to check her pulse. It was there, but reedy and thin. And the blood on her chest had spread in a frightening pattern on her blouse.

He put pressure on her wound, trying to stop the bleeding, gun still held in one hand. As the man on the floor screamed in pain, Hank prayed for Zack to get here in time to save Melody's life.

Chapter 15

"You have to wake up," Lainie said, her voice a sweet familiar sound. "Melody, you have to wake up now."

"But I don't want to leave you," Melody said.

Lainie smiled, that loving gesture that put a sparkle in her eyes and warmed Melody's heart. "I don't need you anymore, Melody. I'm not afraid. But more important, you don't need me anymore."

Melody stared at the sister who had been such an integral part of her life since the day she'd been born. "I don't?" she asked softly.

Lainie nodded. "You're strong, Melody. So much stronger than you think. You're going to be just fine without me. All you need to do is let me go."

"But I'll miss you," Melody protested.

Again Lainie smiled and touched her sister's cheek

with a soft, feathery hand. "And you'll remember me often, with laughter and joy. Kiss Maddie for me. And now, take a deep breath and open your eyes, Melody. Open your eyes."

Her eyes opened and she realized she was in a hospital bed. She frowned in confusion, for a moment her mind pulling a blank as she tried to remember what had brought her here. It was night. She could tell by the hush in the hallway although the lights in her room were on.

She turned her head slightly toward the window and saw Hank. He was asleep in the chair, his handsome features lined with strain and marred by tiny cuts.

Fred. Memory slammed into her and she drew a deep breath, instantly moaning as a sharp pain pierced through her center.

Hank was instantly at her side and took one of her hands in his. "Don't try to sit up," he said. "You have stitches in your side."

"Mike?" she asked.

Hank's eyes transformed from warm and caring to something cold and hard. "If that's the man who stabbed you, then he's in a hospital room down the hall. I had the distinct pleasure of shooting him in the leg."

"What about Fred? He killed her, Hank. He killed Lainie and then he lured me to his house so he could kill me, too."

He squeezed her hand. "Fred is now in Zack's custody and he'll never be a free man again."

She closed her eyes for a moment, trying to process everything that had happened. She opened her eyes and looked at him once again. "What were you doing at Fred's? How did you know I was in trouble?"

"Maddie. Fred's picture was in the morning paper for some grand opening of a mall. Maddie told me she'd seen him going into Lainie's one night, and I knew you'd told me that Fred had told you he'd never been to Lainie's. The inconsistency made me nervous."

"Thank goodness. If you hadn't gotten nervous, I wouldn't be here right now." She shifted positions on the bed and winced with pain. "Am I going to live?"

He smiled and, in the warmth of that smile, she knew she was going to be fine. "You lost a lot of blood and you have ten stitches where Mike stabbed you, but he managed to miss anything vital."

She nodded. She must have fallen asleep, for when she opened her eyes again, morning sunshine poured through the windows and her mother was in a chair next to her bed.

"Mom." Tears sprang to Melody's eyes as she thought of how devastated her mother must be.

Rita leaned forward and gripped her hand tightly, tears in her eyes as well. "Oh, Melody, thank God you're okay." Rita's tears splashed onto her cheeks. "I thought I'd lost you, too."

"I'm fine, Mom. Please don't cry." Melody knew her mother had plenty to cry about. A daughter who'd been murdered, another daughter nearly suffering the same fate and the man she loved responsible for the ugly betrayal. "I know you feel like you've lost everything," Melody began. "I know you'd planned to live out the rest of your life with Fred."

Rita's eyes flashed and the tears vanished instantly. "I hope he rots in prison," she said with a venom Melody had never heard before. "If they decide to electrocute him, I'll volunteer to throw the switch."

"Mom!"

Rita sat back in her chair and drew a deep breath. "Fred had been pressuring me to marry him for years but something always held me back." She frowned thoughtfully. "It wasn't just Lainie or you or anything I can put my finger on. It was just something inside me that refused to agree to have him as my husband. I knew he was ruthless in his business practices, and that bothered me, but he was kind to me. Now when I think about it, my skin tries to crawl right off my body."

Melody knew that feeling well as she thought of the way James O'Donnell had looked at her. "But you're alone now," Melody said softly.

"Nonsense, I've never been alone. I have you and I have my friends. I have my memories. I have me. I'll be fine." She smiled and patted Melody's hand. "All I want right now is for you to heal and have a wonderful life…for me…for Lainie."

Melody realized that she'd underestimated her mother's strength. It had been Fred who had always told her that her mother was too upset to deal with Lainie. It had been Fred who had perpetrated the myth that Rita was weak and needed him to take care of her.

"She's at peace now, Mom. And so am I," Melody said softly.

"I'm glad." Rita stood and leaned over to kiss Melody on the forehead, the gesture evoking a hundred memories of similar kisses from Melody's childhood. "Zack has been waiting for some time to question you. Do you feel up to seeing him now?"

Melody nodded and within minutes her mother was gone and she was reliving the nightmare for Zack. It was still hard to believe that Fred had been so afraid that Lainie would get pregnant, he'd killed her. That wasn't love; that was sickness. James O'Donnell was a garden-variety creep, but Fred had been something much worse, something evil.

Zack finally had all the information he needed and left.

She was alive. The bad guys were where they belonged and she'd only told a little white lie to her mother when she'd said she was at peace. Her stab wound would heal, but it would take much longer for her heart to scar over.

She was the one who had set the rules, a simple summer fling. But in a matter of weeks, her feelings for Hank had spiraled out of her control.

"I brought you flowers." Maddie danced into the hospital room clutching a vase with an arrangement of colorful blossoms. Hank followed just behind her, and at the sight of the two of them Melody's love welled up inside her, making speech impossible.

Maddie set the vase on the table next to the bed, then leaned over and placed a hand on Melody's cheek, her gaze mournful. "Daddy told me a bad man hurt you. Sometimes when I have a tummy ache, Daddy kisses me and it makes me feel better." She leaned forward and planted a slightly sloppy kiss on Melody's cheek. "There, does that feel better?"

"Definitely," Melody replied.

"Daddy says I can only stay a minute because you're supposed to be twelve to be on this floor. We sneaked me in. Grandma's waiting to take me home."

"I'm so glad you came because I was lying here right before you came in and thinking that what I needed more than anything else in the world was a kiss from Maddie," Melody exclaimed.

Maddie smiled. "I don't think that's really what you were thinking but I love you for telling me that."

"You'd better go with Grandma now," Hank said. "I need to have a grown-up talk with Melody."

Melody blew the little girl a kiss as Susan stuck her head in the door. She waved, and then the two of them disappeared. Hank moved to sit in the chair Rita had vacated earlier.

"How are you really doing?" he asked.

"I'm sore, but I'm feeling better, stronger today. Has anyone told you when I can get out of here?"

Hank shook his head. "I imagine the doctor will be in to speak to you sometime this afternoon."

"I'd like to leave as soon as possible." This was the first time they'd talked since their argument, when hurtful words had been flung back and forth. "Hank, I owe you an apology," she said.

He frowned in confusion. "For what?"

"The last time we spoke I was way out of line. I said things that I had no business saying to you."

"And thank God you did," he said. "Oh, I'll admit, at first I was puffed up with self-righteous anger." He smiled. "As I'm sure you were by the things I said to you. But a crazy thing happened in the last couple of days. I started doing a lot of thinking, something I haven't done much of over the last couple of years."

He stood and walked to the window, where he peered outside. With her gaze, she caressed the broad strength of his back, the long leanness of his legs.

He and his daughter had crashed into her life with a force that had been impossible to resist. Just looking at him standing there she felt the magic, that tingle of pleasure in the pit of her stomach, that wave of sweet possibility that soared in her heart.

"You were right, you know." He turned back to look at her but didn't come any closer. "I'm a rancher at heart. When Rebecca died I turned my back on everything good. It felt obscene for me to be happy in any way with her gone. So, I sold the ranch, distanced myself from my daughter and swore that I'd never really be happy again. I took the job as bodyguard because I didn't care about my life, because deep down inside I was on a road to self-destruction." He laughed and shook his head. "I can see it all so clearly now, and I couldn't see it at all before you yelled at me."

He walked back across the room and sat once again in the chair at her side. "I called Dalton this morning, told him I'm out of the bodyguard business."

"Hank, I'm so glad," she said. If her only role in his life was that of a wake-up call that would bring happiness to both him and Maddie, then she supposed she could live with that.

"I'm going to buy another ranch, become the cowboy my daughter has missed. You gave me my life back,

Melody, and I'll never be able to thank you enough for it." His eyes glowed and she forced a smile to her lips while her heart cried out with her love for him.

"I'm glad, Hank. You and Maddie deserve all the happiness in the world."

"You know, I thought I was a bodyguard in training, but in truth I was a man in training and I think with your help, I've graduated."

At that moment Dr. Fedor walked in. "Ah, you look much better today than you did the last time I checked on you," he said to Melody. "Hank, if you'll just step outside, I need to check my handiwork."

"I'll talk to you later," Hank said and disappeared out the door.

Dr. Fedor pulled back the sheet and kept up a running stream of friendly chatter as he gently removed the bandage across her wound.

"Things look good," he said. "You're going to have a scar, but it shouldn't be too bad and will certainly fade with time."

"That's good," Melody said and burst into tears.

"Did I hurt you?" Dr. Fedor asked worriedly.

She shook her head as the sobs continued. "I'm fine," she managed to say. "I'm just overly emotional."

Dr. Fedor hurriedly covered her back up again. "It's no wonder you're feeling weepy. You've been through quite an ordeal. Do you need a tranquilizer? Something to calm you down?"

"No, no, I'll be fine," she replied. There was no point in correcting him. There was no reason to tell him that having a man almost kill her wasn't why she was crying.

She was crying because Hank and Maddie were going to have a wonderful life. She was crying because that wonderful life didn't include her.

Hank stood at the window of his unit, watching as Melody got out of her mother's car. He hadn't been back to the hospital since the day before when they'd been interrupted by the doctor. He'd hoped that she'd call him if she was released from the hospital and needed a ride home, but obviously she'd called her mother.

It was finally over. Lainie's murder had been solved and now Melody would be making plans to get back to her life in Chicago. He would always be grateful to her. She'd given him back his life, but the emptiness that ached in him as he thought of her being gone had nothing to do with gratefulness.

Within minutes Rita reappeared, got into her car and took off. Hank frowned. Surely she hadn't left her daughter, fresh out of the hospital, alone in a town house that had few amenities? But it looked like that's exactly what she'd done.

Dammit, why hadn't she gone home with her mother? She needed care and attention. She could be so stubborn! Even though he told himself it was none of his business, that *she* was none of his business anymore, he found himself stalking down the hallway to Lainie's front door.

He didn't knock, nor was the door locked. He walked inside and called her name. "Back here," she called from the bedroom.

She sat on the side of the twin bed in the guest room

and she smiled as he appeared in the doorway. He didn't return the gesture. "What in the hell are you doing back here?" he asked. He didn't give her an opportunity to answer. "You need to be someplace where somebody can take care of you."

"I've taken care of myself just fine all my life," she replied.

"You have stitches, and you still have bruised ribs. You shouldn't be here alone. What was your mother thinking, just dropping you off and driving away?" He stared at her in frustration, knowing she was probably going to fire back at him with both barrels. Instead she laughed, then winced, then laughed again.

"I think what Mom was thinking was that she'd go pick up the prescriptions that are waiting for me at the drugstore while I gathered my things up here so I could go back home with her."

Hank stepped back, feeling like a total fool. And in that moment, he knew what emotion had caused him to stomp over here, recognized what he'd known deep inside for a while. He loved Melody Thompson.

The realization struck him like a blow to the gut and brought with it an incredible sense of joy and a fierce pang of pain. He loved her, and soon she would be gone.

"Are you all right?" she asked, pulling him from his tortured thoughts.

"Yeah…no. No, I'm not all right. I'm scared," he said in a low voice. He'd never confessed to being scared about anything to anyone before.

She got up from the bed, her eyes the glorious blue that pierced his heart. "Scared? Scared of what?"

He gazed at her, seeing the tender concern on her features, remembering not only making love with her, but laughing with her and talking about things that mattered and things that didn't.

"I'm scared of letting you go," he finally said. "You brought me back to life, you made me fall in love with you and now you're going to leave to go back to your life and I can't imagine not having you here with me and Maddie."

She stood perfectly still, as if his words had frozen her to stone, and he continued, unable to stop himself. "I know you have a job teaching in Chicago, but surely they need teachers around these parts, too. I don't know how you feel about living on a ranch, but there's nothing that would make Maddie happier than having you as a stepmother." He finally stopped talking, wondering if his words had been a futile effort.

She took a step closer to him, her features giving nothing away. "Your mother told me that you had magic with Rebecca. I feel magic with you, Hank, but I need to know if that's what you feel with me." Her eyes grew misty, as if she feared what his answer might be.

He carefully pulled her into his arms, needing to touch her, smell her. "Whenever I hear your voice, I feel happy. Looking at you makes me need to touch you, to hold you. And spending time with you makes me want to be the best man that I can be. I'd call that magic, wouldn't you?"

A sweet sigh escaped her and she leaned into him, her head on his chest as his arms enfolded her. "I love you, Hank. I didn't mean to fall in love with you, but I did."

"Then marry me. Be my wife, Melody. Let's build a future together starting today. Rebecca was my magic in the past, but you're my magic for my future."

She raised her head to gaze at him, her eyes shining with the light of her love for him. It humbled him, that he would find this kind of love, this kind of magic twice in his lifetime. "Yes," she said softly and he dipped his head to claim her lips with his.

"Daddy?" Maddie burst into the bedroom and the two adults sprang apart. Maddie stared from one to the other. "Daddy, you were kissing Melody. You were kissing her on the lips."

"I guess I was," he agreed with a wide smile. "I always kiss the woman I'm going to marry on the lips."

Maddie's eyes widened. "For real? If you marry her then she'll be my new mommy."

"Then I guess you're going to get a new mommy," Hank replied. He and Melody laughed as Maddie squealed her delight. "And we're going to find a nice ranch to live on," he added.

Happy tears dampened Maddie's eyes. "My dream is coming true," she exclaimed.

"Mine, too," Melody said with a long, loving look at Hank.

"You know what I think?" Maddie asked. "I think Lainie and Mommy are smiling at us from heaven."

"I think you're right," Melody replied and smiled as Hank pulled his two best girls into his arms.

"All I know is right now I'm the happiest man on the face of the earth," he said.

Melody smiled at him, a teasing glint in her eyes.

"You started out as a bodyguard in training and you're going from that to being a husband in training."

"I like the sound of that," he said, and as Maddie clapped her approval he captured Melody's lips once again in a kiss that held all his heart, all his soul and the magic of love.

* * * * *

Chapter 1

October
New York City

Nicole Masters was sitting cross-legged on her sofa while a cold autumn rain peppered the windows of her fourth-floor apartment. She was poking at the ice cream in her bowl and trying not to be in a mood.

Six weeks ago, a simple trip to her neighborhood pharmacy had turned into a nightmare. She'd walked into the middle of a robbery. She never even saw the man who shot her in the head and left her for dead. She'd survived, but some of her senses had not. She was dealing with short-term memory loss and a tendency to stagger. Even though she'd been told the problems were most likely temporary, she waged a daily battle with depression.

Her parents had been killed in a car wreck when she was twenty-one. And except for a few friends—and most recently her boyfriend, Dominic Tucci, who lived in the apartment right above hers—she was alone. Her doctor kept reminding her that she should be grateful to be alive, and on one level she knew he was right. But he wasn't living in her shoes.

If she'd been anywhere else but at that pharmacy when the robbery happened, she wouldn't have died twice on the way to the hospital. Instead of being grateful that she'd survived, she couldn't stop thinking of what she'd lost.

But that wasn't the end of her troubles. On top of everything else, something strange was happening inside her head. She'd begun to hear odd things: sounds, not voices—at least, she didn't think it was voices. It was more like the distant noise of rapids—a rush of wind and water inside her head that, when it came, blocked out everything around her. It didn't happen often, but when it did, it was frightening, and it was driving her crazy.

The blank moments, which is what she called them, even had a rhythm. First there came that sound, then a cold sweat, then panic with no reason. Part of her feared it was the beginning of an emotional breakdown. And part of her feared it wasn't—that it was going to turn out to be a permanent souvenir of her resurrection.

Frustrated with herself and the situation as it stood, she upped the sound on the TV remote. But instead of *Wheel of Fortune,* an announcer broke in with a special bulletin.

"This just in. Police are on the scene of a kidnapping that occurred only hours ago at The Dakota. Molly Dane, the six-year-old daughter of one of Hollywood's blockbuster stars, Lyla Dane, was taken by force from the family apartment. At this time they have yet to receive a ransom demand. The housekeeper was seriously injured during the abduction, and is, at the present time, in surgery. Police are hoping to be able to talk to her once she regains consciousness. In the meantime, we are going now to a press conference with Lyla Dane."

Horrified, Nicole stilled as the cameras went live to where the actress was speaking before a bank of microphones. The shock and terror in Lyla Dane's voice were physically painful to watch. But even though Nicole kept upping the volume, the sound continued to fade.

Just when she was beginning to think something was wrong with her set, the broadcast suddenly switched from the Dane press conference to what appeared to be footage of the kidnapping, beginning with footage from inside the apartment.

When the front door suddenly flew back against the wall and four men rushed in, Nicole gasped. Horrified, she quickly realized that this must have been caught on a security camera inside the Dane apartment.

As Nicole continued to watch, a small Asian woman, who she guessed was the maid, rushed forward in an effort to keep them out. When one of the men hit her in the face with his gun, Nicole moaned. The violence was too reminiscent of what she'd lived through. Sick to her stomach, she fisted her hands against her belly, wishing it was over, but unable to tear her gaze away.

When the maid dropped to the carpet, the same man followed with a vicious kick to the little woman's midsection that lifted her off the floor.

"Oh, my God," Nicole said. When blood began to pool beneath the maid's head, she started to cry.

As the tape played on, the four men split up in different directions. The camera caught one running down a long marble hallway, then disappearing into a room. Moments later he reappeared, carrying a little girl, who Nicole assumed was Molly Dane. The child was wearing a pair of red pants and a white turtleneck sweater, and her hair was partially blocking her abductor's face as he carried her down the hall. She was kicking and screaming in his arms, and when he slapped her, it elicited an agonized scream that brought the other three running. Nicole watched in horror as one of them ran up and put his hand over Molly's face. Seconds later, she went limp.

One moment they were in the foyer, then they were gone.

Nicole jumped to her feet, then staggered drunkenly. The bowl of ice cream she'd absentmindedly placed in her lap shattered at her feet, splattering glass and melting ice cream everywhere.

The picture on the screen abruptly switched from the kidnapping to what Nicole assumed was a rerun of Lyla Dane's plea for her daughter's safe return, but she was numb.

Before she could think what to do next, the doorbell

rang. Startled by the unexpected sound, she shakily swiped at the tears and took a step forward. She didn't feel the glass shards piercing her feet until she took the second step. At that point, sharp pains shot through her foot. She gasped, then looked down in confusion. Her legs looked as if she'd been running through mud, and she was standing in broken glass and ice cream, while a thin ribbon of blood seeped out from beneath her toes.

"Oh, no," Nicole mumbled, then stifled a second moan of pain.

The doorbell rang again. She shivered, then clutched her head in confusion.

"Just a minute!" she yelled, then tried to sidestep the rest of the debris as she hobbled to the door.

When she looked through the peephole in the door, she didn't know whether to be relieved or regretful.

It was Dominic, and as usual, she was a mess.

Nicole smiled a little self-consciously as she opened the door to let him in. "I just don't know what's happening to me. I think I'm losing my mind."

"Hey, don't talk about my woman like that."

Nicole rode the surge of delight his words brought. "So I'm still your woman?"

Dominic lowered his head.

Their lips met.

The kiss proceeded.

Slowly.

Thoroughly.

* * * * *

Be sure to look for the
AFTERSHOCK *anthology next month, as
well as other exciting paranormal stories
from Silhouette Nocturne.
Available in October wherever books are sold.*

nocturne™

NEW YORK TIMES BESTSELLING AUTHOR

SHARON SALA

JANIS REAMES HUDSON
DEBRA COWAN

AFTERSHOCK

Three women are brought to the brink of death...
only to discover the aftershock of their trauma has
left them with unexpected and unwelcome gifts of
paranormal powers. Now each woman must learn to
accept her newfound abilities while fighting for life,
love and second chances....

Available October wherever books are sold.

www.eHarlequin.com
www.paranormalromanceblog.wordpress.com   SN61796

REQUEST YOUR FREE BOOKS!

2 FREE NOVELS PLUS 2 FREE GIFTS!

Silhouette® Romantic

SUSPENSE

Sparked by Danger, Fueled by Passion!

YES! Please send me 2 FREE Silhouette® Romantic Suspense novels and my 2 FREE gifts (gifts are worth about $10). After receiving them, if I don't wish to receive any more books, I can return the shipping statement marked "cancel." If I don't cancel, I will receive 4 brand-new novels every month and be billed just $4.24 per book in the U.S. or $4.99 per book in Canada, plus 25¢ shipping and handling per book plus applicable taxes, if any*. That's a savings of at least 15% off the cover price! I understand that accepting the 2 free books and gifts places me under no obligation to buy anything. I can always return a shipment and cancel at any time. Even if I never buy another book from Silhouette, the two free books and gifts are mine to keep forever.

240 SDN EEX6 340 SDN EEYJ

Name	(PLEASE PRINT)	

Address		Apt. #

City	State/Prov.	Zip/Postal Code

Signature (if under 18, a parent or guardian must sign)

Mail to the Silhouette Reader Service:
IN U.S.A.: P.O. Box 1867, Buffalo, NY 14240-1867
IN CANADA: P.O. Box 609, Fort Erie, Ontario L2A 5X3

Not valid to current subscribers of Silhouette Romantic Suspense books.

Want to try two free books from another line?
Call 1-800-873-8635 or visit www.morefreebooks.com.

* Terms and prices subject to change without notice. N.Y. residents add applicable sales tax. Canadian residents will be charged applicable provincial taxes and GST. Offer not valid in Quebec. This offer is limited to one order per household. All orders subject to approval. Credit or debit balances in a customer's account(s) may be offset by any other outstanding balance owed by or to the customer. Please allow 4 to 6 weeks for delivery. Offer available while quantities last.

Your Privacy: Silhouette is committed to protecting your privacy. Our Privacy Policy is available online at www.eHarlequin.com or upon request from the Reader Service. From time to time we make our lists of customers available to reputable third parties who may have a product or service of interest to you. If you would prefer we not share your name and address, please check here. ☐

SRS08R

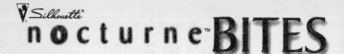

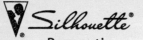
Silhouette® Romantic
SUSPENSE

COMING NEXT MONTH

#1531 UNDERCOVER WIFE—Merline Lovelace
Code Name: Danger
Rough around the edges Mike Callahan, code name Hawkeye, objects
when he's paired with sophisticated Gillian Ridgeway on a dangerous spy
mission to Hong Kong. Hawk is an overprotective man with a wounded
past, and Gillian has secretly been in love with him for years. Now the two
must put their lives—and hearts—at risk for each other.

#1532 RANCHER'S REDEMPTION—Beth Cornelison
The Coltons: Family First
Rancher Clay Colton discovers a wrecked car and a bag of money on his
property, so the local police call in a CSI team—headed by his ex-wife,
Tamara. As she investigates, the two are thrown into the path of danger,
uncovering secrets about the crime as well as their true feelings for each
other.

#1533 TERMS OF SURRENDER—Kylie Brant
Alpha Squad
Targeted by a bank robber bent on revenge, hostage negotiators and former
lovers Dace Recker and Jolie Conrad are reunited against their will. The
FBI has recruited them to draw out the killer, but their close proximity to
each other will draw out wounds from their past. Can they heal their hearts
for a second chance at love?

#1534 THE DOCTOR'S MISSION—Lyn Stone
Special Ops
When Dr. Nick Sandro is recruited to help COMPASS agent Cate Olin
recover after a head injury, his mission is complicated by the feelings they
still harbor for each other. Escaping to Tuscany as a terrorist sends men
after Cate, Nick must do all he can to protect her. But they'll have to work
together to destroy the final threat.

SRSCNM0908